Love Fumbles 2:

A Coming of Age Novel about Perseverance, Race, and Relationships

By Regina N. Smith

Disclaimer

Copyright 2021 © by Regina N. Smith

All Rights Reserved

Cover art design by Elena Dudina

https://www.elenadudina.com/

For

My husband, SSG (US Army) Kenneth M.
Klimowitz (Ret.), who served as the inspiration
for Paul during his military career

and

My mother, Lillie B. Smith

Prologue

Paul, 1963

It was moving day, a time to say goodbye, and a day of holding onto the memories. That was all that was left, excluding the thick book of pictures that eleven-year-old Paul Boudreaux had in his hand. The picture book held some of his memories: birthday parties, past Christmases, and other social events that he held dear with his parents. It was only yesterday that the good times had ended, when he heard of his parents' unfortunate accident in Wood Oak, Louisiana.

Yesterday, Paul had returned home from playing another weekend baseball game with his friends when he came home to an empty house. Usually, he would have been greeted by his mother, Helen Boudreaux, a forty-year-old socialite with black hair and hazel eyes. Often the talk of the parish, Helen was known for her attractiveness, weekly luncheons, and sponsorships for the less fortunate in the community. Kindhearted, as Helen was, it was that which broke Paul's heart the most, to never be able to feel the tenderness of his mother's warm embrace ever again.

Paul's father, Andrew Boudreaux, a forty-five-year-old, community oriented, businessman with black hair and grey eyes had an idyllic reputation within the small parish. Paul's grandfather, Abraham, had given each of his sons their inheritances years ago, which included money and properties, intending to see how prosperous each son would become. Andrew was given Sal's Country Store and a lump sum of money. With his assets, he began to expand and remodel the store, hiring those whom he felt needed the extra financial support. Therefore, gaining the respect of the Wood Oak community. His fortune grew, unlike his brothers who eventually lost everything due to addictions of gambling or terrible investments. In secret, the men began making secret deals with Andrew ultimately gaining possession of all the properties, including their homes, in exchange for financial relief, hoping Abraham would never discover their missteps.

Paul had been Andrew and Helen's miracle child, after many years of unsuccessful attempts of trying to conceive. Now, an orphan, Paul had a new guardian, his grandfather, Abraham Boudreaux, one of the most feared men in the area. For an elderly man in his late sixties, Abraham was well built, and his grey eyes had an austere gaze. His grey hair was neatly groomed in a professional contour style, and his suit consisted of a black necktie, white shirt that was buttoned under a solid dark grey tailor-made jacket and pants. His freshly polished black shoes shimmered in the sunlight.

Paul held the book closer to his plaid yellow and green shirt. His solid green pants partially covered his brown shoes. His black hair was brushed to the back in a trendy ducktail hairstyle. His grey eyes stared at the doorstep. His posture was stooped with lowered shoulders that only dropped further as he picked up one of the full suitcases.

Paul lifted his head to see his grandfather, Abraham, finish locking the door to the house that Paul once called home with the turn of a key and stuffing it into his front pocket. For the first time in his life, Paul could see a glimmer of anguish in his grandfather's eyes. Then, as if burying his moment of vulnerability, Abraham cleared his throat and gazed at the top of the outside door frame.

"This is no longer your home," his grandfather said with his deep, heavy voice. "Your new home will be with me, down the street."

The elderly man picked up two of the suitcases and began his stride down the porch steps. Quickly, Paul followed Abraham to his new home, the biggest and widest two-story house on the street.

Once there, Abraham unlocked the door to his home, a lavish, well-furnished house with both antique and modern furniture. It had five bedrooms, with one being a guestroom and one still occupied by Abraham. The other rooms, long abandoned by Abraham's adult sons were still adorned in the same manner that each had left them many years ago.

Paul trailed Abraham upstairs to the last room on the right, at the end of the hallway. Paul knew which room he would be living in: his father's. It was tidy with his *father's old shirts and pants from his teenage years still hanging in the closet. An old leather baseball glove and baseball sat on top of the dresser next to a small playfully arranged set of tiny metallic cars. There was a small desk and chair with a clock, lamp, radio, and an open book from an unfinished reading. On the wall were green and white pennants from his father's old high school, Wood Oak High School.*

Placing the two suitcases on the floor, Abraham walked out of the room, leaving Paul. Paul placed the suitcase he was carrying next to the ones his grandfather left. He put the photo album on the bed and sat down next to it, not desiring to unpack anything. He was not home. Home was a still a few houses down the street, the place that was now locked. Paul wanted to tell his grandfather to give him back his old house key, to open his parents' home and be greeted by the familiar faces that he knew loved him. Hopeless, Paul lingered in the room, hearing the phone ringing downstairs and his grandfather's angry voice bellowing below.

"Paul will be living with me from this moment on and I will handle his father's affairs," Abraham stated, his voice incensed over the phone, "Reinvest? Reinvest in what? So, you can take all the money Andrew worked hard for and lose that too? Did you think that I would never find out about the deal you and Philip made with Andrew, selling him the deeds to your properties to make up for your mistakes? I have all of Andrew's papers right here,

along with your deed! You thought you were being clever thinking your brother would bail you out of all your mess and now that he is gone, all should be forgiven, and everything returned to you. Well, the buck stops here. Andrew is gone and the days of him holding your hand are finished. If you want your house back, you will have to purchase it back, even if it takes you working at Sal's until the day before your death, seeing that nobody else is willing to hire you for even the simplest of tasks. Until you have the money, you will be nothing more than a mere employee at Sal's Country Store."

Chapter 1

Paul, 1970

Peering from behind the tall pine trees, the glorious sun rose from its slumber. It was a new day and for the weary travelers, a new beginning. The once frigid air grew warm, as if kissed by the sun, bringing a mild tenderness to its disgruntled inhabitants below.

Snapping out of his daydreams, seventeen-year-old, Paul Boudreaux winced, pressing his fingers against his throbbing forehead. His headache persisted and his jaw was still aching from hours before. Clutching onto parts of his short black hair, he struggled to fight back the discomfort, closing his dark grey eyes. Paul's yellow and blue plaid shirt, blue jeans, and brown leather shoes had tiny remnants of blood and debris. What started out as a beautiful evening the night before turned into a nightmare hours ago.

Paul's cousin, seventeen-year-old, Bill Boudreaux, sure gave it to him good. Bill did what was anticipated, knocking someone out with one punch of his fist. Unfortunately, this time, Paul was on the receiving end of Bill's wrath. It was no surprise why most students at Wood Oak High School would be caught flinching or dispersing whenever he was around. Fortunately, for Paul, Bill was no longer around, for the time being, and the least of his worries.

Aside from his own discomforts, Paul's concerns were focused on his girlfriend, Nell Jefferson, a seventeen-year-old Negro female who Paul had been exposed to having a secret relationship with, forcing them to flee from his grandfather's Klan organization, The Family. Where they were presently, Paul had no idea, but they were safe.

I'm sorry, Paul wanted to say to his girlfriend, but with each attempt, the words would choke in his throat. He reached down, giving Nell's hand a gentle squeeze.

Nell appeared nauseous, removing her hand from Paul's to wrap around her stomach. Leaning forward, Nell began to squint her deep brown eyes. She let out a muffled whimper while loose strands of her short black hair fell forward. Nell's clothing, which consisted of a white sweater, purple and white dress and white shoes, also had small remnants of dirt and dried blood. She began gagging, immediately covering her mouth with her hand.

Anxious, Paul turned towards the front of the car, driven by his childhood friend, Henry Wilkerson. Seventeen-year-old Henry Wilkerson had red hair, blue eyes, and pale skin covered in freckles. He wore a plaid yellow and brown shirt, solid blue jeans, and brown hunting boots. Next to him was his rifle, empty of bullets. Henry was livid and his freckled hands grasped the steering wheel tightly. There was tension in his eyes, especially when they fell upon *her* when he would sneak a glance from his rear-view mirror. Overtly, Henry blamed

Nell for everyone turning against Paul and being the cause of their unexpected departure. Henry's lips would curl or flatten, and his face began to turn the reddest that Paul had ever seen. The entire sour mood of everyone in the vehicle was growing at a rapid rate.

"Could you pull over?" Paul asked Henry, his voice strained.

Silent, Henry veered his vehicle over to the side of the road, ending the drive. Instantaneously, Nell flung the car's back passenger door open, rushing outside, and gagging. Paul and Henry knew why, but out of everyone there, Henry could care less about Nell and *her problems*.

"This is insane," Henry protested, snorting, and spitting out the driver's car window. "Why am *I* driving *her* around, like she is some kind of big shot? How do you even know it's *your* kid? It could be anybody's! All the times you did it with Nancy, she never ended knocked up. I bet Nell has been lying the entire time to string you along. Neither of us should have to deal with her. Just say the word and we are out of here! Someone else can pick her up and deal with her nonsense."

"Knock it off, will you," Paul stated, opening the other passenger door. "*We* are not leaving her behind, at least, *I'm* not. Just drop us off at the next town and she and I can leave."

"I'm not leaving you with her," Henry retorted. "We can still go to my great aunt's place in Florida and start all over. Bringing Nell along is going to bring us nothing but problems. She turned the entire parish against you! Do you want to be chased out of every town to be with her? Nell doesn't care about you! She's only protecting herself or worse yet, using you for your money."

"Yeah, well, what about *you* and the lynch mob that *you* were a part of?" Paul fired back. "Care to explain *that*, pal? Why didn't you warn me before joining the others at the cabin?"

"*I* didn't have anything to do with what happened at the cabin," Henry explained. "If you remember correctly, several of the guys and I asked if you wanted to go hunting with us earlier yesterday and you said you were busy. So, we all went hunting without you! When we were on our way back home, we were flagged down by Mr. Nelson who told us that the Family had an emergency meeting at your family's cabin. We all assumed that you would be there. I searched for you once we got there, but you weren't around, so I will admit that I snuck into the cabin through an open window to take a leak. It's not like I could just whip it out with all the women and kids around! Then on my way out, I saw your uncle's vehicle pull up with all of you in it and him flappin' his lip about you and *her*. I was shocked like everyone else and knew you were done for, especially when your uncle convinced everyone to get rid of you because you knew too much about everyone. I had to rush back to my car and get my rifle and bullets to help get you out of your mess. That was a dumb move you made, getting involved with any colored girl. You should have stuck with out with Nancy or better yet, Brenda Miller and her huge tits!"

Giving up, Paul threw up his hands and slammed them back down on his thighs. *If Henry liked Brenda Miller and her tits so bad, he could have dated her himself.* Paul did not feel like arguing with Henry to explain why he loved his girlfriend who was three months pregnant and wasn't going to leave her. He was emotionally, physically, and mentally exhausted. Knowing how hardheaded Henry was, the debate could go around in multiple circles, making the situation worse with both guys wanting to pound each other.

"Let's talk about this later," Paul suggested, desiring to disengage from the conversation. "I need to get some air and check on Nell." He departed from the car, hoping to sooth his frayed nerves. Paul walked towards Nell, nearing the tall pine trees where she was hunched over grabbing her sides. Near her feet was the vomit she had expelled. As Nell rose from her stooped posture, Paul wrapped his arms around her, praying that it would provide a little bit of comfort to her between the tears that were beginning to brim from her eyes.

Disregarding the affection the lovebirds had towards each other, Henry switched off the car engine and rolled up the car window. He lifted his rifle from the front passenger seat and walked to the back of the automobile. Unlocking the trunk, he placed the rifle inside and reentered the driver's seat of the car, slamming the door. He yawned, rubbing his sleepy eyes. He had driven most of the night and was sleepy. Closing his eyes, Henry folded his arms across his chest, waiting for the passengers to return.

"Babe, are you okay?" Paul addressed Nell, still outside in their embrace.

Smiling weakly, Nell nodded, averting her gaze to her sweater pockets. She pulled out two peppermints, popping one into her mouth. She offered Paul one, which he gratefully accepted.

"I'm sorry about what happened in Wood Oak," Paul said. "I didn't know that any of that was going to happen and neither did Henry. We should be far enough from Wood Oak to be safe for now. Once we get closer to a phone booth, we can contact your family and let them know where you are."

"But what about you, Paul?" Nell inquired. "You took a huge hit and was knocked out for a while. We should take you to a hospital."

"I'll be fine," Paul assured her. "What matters is that we all are safe. Henry's been driving all night, so I'm going to drive for a little bit while he rests. You should get some rest too." They both walked back to the car. Paul knocked on the front window, waking Henry. "You got the keys to the car? I'll drive us to the next town."

Yawning, Henry handed Paul his car keys, scooting over into the front passenger seat, and shutting his eyes again. Nell climbed into the back passenger seat of the automobile, closing the door behind her. Sliding into the driver's seat, Paul restarted the car, and continued driving along the interstate.

Chapter 2

Resuming their drive along the interstate, Paul spotted a parish designation sign that revealed that they were nearing a small rural community called, Magnolia, Louisiana. Famished, Paul drove off the interstate onto the highway towards the rural area. *Surely, there must be places where the locals go to eat, shop, or have fun.*

The automobile drove past several plantation fields being run by sharecroppers. There were sugarcane mills and farmlands where cattle, hogs, chickens, and pigs grazed. Along the main highway were paved and dirt roads where men labored, digging ditches. Further along, near the sides of the roads, were trucks and cars with people selling cabbages, corn, catfish, chickens, and other items.

"Mmm," Paul sighed, "It's early, but, I wish I had some of that corn with some melted butter."

"And catfish," Nell added, beaming, "with some homemade tartar sauce would hit the spot."

Further into Magnolia there were shopping centers that sold sweets, clothing, shoe repair services, and grocery stores. Other buildings consisted of a bowling alley, schools, churches, family restaurants, and a drive-in movie theater. Behind the shops and eateries were shotgun houses and adjacent neighborhoods.

Unexpectedly, Henry's car began to make jerking movements, refocusing Paul and Nell's attention from their empty stomachs back onto their mode of transportation. Paul clinched his jaw and parked the vehicle into the parking lot of a nearby eatery. The cool air to the car stopped blowing, forcing Paul to roll down the window.

"Come on," Paul grumbled. He attempted to restart the automobile by turning the key in the ignition switch, but nothing happened. It completely stopped.

"What's wrong?" Nell asked.

"That's what I'd like to know," Paul responded, examining the dashboard. He nudged Henry with his elbow, waking his friend. "Something's wrong with the car... It stopped working."

"Oh, crap, I forgot about the stupid gas gage being broken," Henry confessed, cringing, and partially covering his face with his hand. "Chances are that's what it is: us running out of gas. I meant to say something earlier, but I was so tired that I forgot!"

Paul lowered his chin to his chest, slowly shaking his head. The day was hardly commencing and already they were having calamities: if the car needed fuel, the nearest station was a lengthy distance up the road. To make sure that the lack of fuel was indeed the problem, Paul directed for everyone to get out of the vehicle. Once everyone was out, Paul took the car's gas cap off. Listening, he began to rock the car back and forth. There was no slush sound, meaning there was no more gas in the vehicle. Paul placed the gas cap back on and shook his head at Henry.

Reentering the automobile, everyone remained quiet. Henry didn't have to say anything for Paul to know how his pal was feeling: guilty and it was evident by his silence alone compared to his boisterous and wild personality. Nell leaned against the car door with her hand pressed against her forehead. She had a pinched, tension filled expression upon her face. Paul tilted his head back against the driver's seat, pondering for a way to make their situation less dire. The only thing that wasn't awful was the delicious aroma coming from the restaurant whose parking lot they were stuck in.

I'm so hungry I can't even think straight, Paul thought. Whatever they are cooking in there sure does smell good. I'm going to go in and order us something to eat. First, I need to make sure that this is a safe place. Second, I don't think I can leave Henry alone with Nell. He is too much of a loose cannon and not many people can handle him like I can. It would be better if I just take him with me.

"You hungry, pal?" Paul questioned Henry.

"You don't have to ask me twice," Henry responded, withdrawing from the vehicle. He began dragging his hands through his red hair repeatedly.

Paul eyed Nell. *I don't see anyone else around the parking lot, so you should be safe for now. Henry and I will go inside, look at the menu, order, and hurry back. This shouldn't take long.*

"Wait here, babe," Paul instructed Nell. "We will be back soon." He followed Henry into the parking lot. Paul speculated what delectable items would be served in the restaurant. It had been a while since he had some pancakes drizzled with maple syrup, or better yet, French toast with a thick slice of bacon or ham off to the side. His mouth began to water, thinking of the succulent taste the different food items would bring to his tastebuds.

Suddenly, Henry stopped in his tracks and put his arm out, blocking Paul's path. His face paled. Paul's eyes followed Henry's gaze to a laughing small group of people departing the establishment. It was a group of Negro people that were chuckling and joking around, heading back to their cars. Henry gawked at the sign at the top of the restaurant that read, "Leroy's." Immediately, Henry spun around, going back towards his vehicle.

"Where are you going?" Paul asked him. "I thought you were hungry."

"No way," Henry spat. "I'm heading back. Go in by yourself if you want to."

Paul lingered by himself. A Negro man departing the restaurant briefly locked eyes with him but recommenced his walk towards his own automobile. Paul's mouth grew dry, and his facial muscles began to tic. He noticed more Negro people leaving the eatery, making him assume that he was at a place where people like him weren't welcomed. If Magnolia was anything like Wood Oak, people stayed in their own areas, and he was out of his. It would be easier to go back to Henry's car and go somewhere else, but where to? They were in an unfamiliar place with hardly any money between them. Who knew if the next few restaurants would be the same? Where would that leave him? Paul had never been to a Negro restaurant in his life, much less one by himself. Who was he to enter their business and ask anything of them? Turning around, Paul went back to Henry's car.

Henry was in the front passenger seat, his head tossed back, and his arms folded across his chest. He was dozing off and was beginning to snore.

Nell was in her same slumped position, leaning against the car door. Things were back to square one.

"I have to go to the bathroom," Nell informed Paul once he opened the backseat door.

You've got to be kidding me, Paul thought moving aside while Nell scooted herself from the vehicle. He slumped against the car, rubbing his fingertips at the middle of his forehead while his eyes were closed.

"What's wrong?" Nell questioned him. "Is this another prejudiced place, like the ones in Wood Oak?"

"U-uh," Paul stammered, opening his eyes. "I don't know… I've never been here before. It seems to be an… all-colored place."

"Oh," was all that escaped Nell's lips. She raised an eyebrow and tilted her head. Briefly, she crossed her arms and stood in a wide stance before giving him a harsh squint. Without another word, Nell sauntered past Paul, towards the building.

"Wait," Paul called out, taking off behind her. "Don't be mad at me! I didn't mean to sound offensive! We don't know what it's like in there!"

"It must be decent if it has plenty of vehicles parked in the parking lot," Nell refuted, halting her walk. "If *you* don't feel comfortable, *I* can just bring *you* something back."

"I can't let you go into a strange place by yourself! I don't want anything to happen to you!"

"Where else am I supposed to go, huh? Into an all-white restaurant as a Negro woman where anything can happen there too? Regardless of where we go, one of us going to be uncomfortable. Least here I can use the bathroom in peace."

Nell began moving again. Swearing under his breath, Paul went with her into the restaurant. His chest began to tighten before the door had an opportunity to fully close. Jazz music from an old juke box complimented the eatery, along with the wonderful aroma of food being prepared from the kitchen. The restaurant was snug with booths and tables that were nearly filled with a mixture of young families and elderly customers, who were either kidding around or deep within their own conversations. Everyone in the establishment was Negro, except for Paul. Then, the expected occurred. The laughing and joshing at most of the tables ceased when they spotted Paul. Their curious eyes began watching and studying him, increasing his anxieties.

Finding an empty booth near the window, Nell mouthed for Paul to follow her. Each step seeming heavier than the last, Paul complied. At the table, they sat across from one another. Beads of sweat began to form on Paul's forehead as he struggled to not cover his face with his hand, forcing it underneath the table.

This is so awkward, Paul thought. *Why can't everyone just turn around and stop staring at me like I'm some kind of ghost.*

A young waitress, in her early twenties, approached their booth. She had dark brown skin and eyes and a medium black afro. On her solid white blouse, there was a name tag that read, *Tracy.* Additionally, she had a red and white checkered apron, solid brown pants and white tennis shoes. Clearing her throat, Tracy handed the two teens restaurant menus. She pulled out a small writing pad and black pen from her apron pocket.

"Welcome to Leroy's," Tracy introduced herself, "My name is Tracy. What can I get you to drink?"

"Orange juice for me," Nell answered. "Could you please tell me where the bathroom is."

"It's that way towards the back, last door on the left," Tracy replied nodding towards the back of the establishment.

"Thank you," Nell said, getting out of her seat and leaving Paul with the waitress.

Paul stared at the menu, lifting it to cover his uneasy face. *So, this is how Nell and Martin must have felt on their first day at Wood Oak High School. What a terrible feeling! I am so ashamed of how me and the other students acted back then! If I had a chance to do things over, I would have done more to make them feel more comfortable and welcomed. I'm such a jerk!*

"And you?" Tracy questioned him, breaking Paul away from his thoughts. "What can I get you to drink?"

"Orange juice," Paul replied, his throat seemingly constricted.

Tracy jotted the order on her pad and left the booth. Gradually, people began to turn away from Paul, recommencing their own dining or conversations. Nell returned to the table and picked up her menu. Paul checked his menu, reading what was offered: bacon, eggs, grits, biscuits, French toast, cinnamon rolls, etc. Everything sounded delectable and was reasonably priced. When Tracy came back with the drinks, both teens settled on a breakfast of French toast and bacon for themselves, and a cinnamon roll and cup of orange juice to go for Henry, since he refused to go inside and order for himself.

With their breakfast on the table, Paul gawked at Nell's plate, his lips curling with revulsion. Nell had cut up her French toast and bacon, picking at it with her fork before dunking the bits into her orange juice, and eating it between sips.

"What in the world are you doing?" Paul questioned her, after making a choking noise in his throat.

"Eating my food, like everybody else," Nell responded, stuffing more of the weird mixture into her mouth.

Nobody is eating their food like you are, Paul wanted to say. He dug his fork into his French toast, resuming his eating.

The restaurant was thinning out and there were *clangs* and *bings* of dishes and silverware being collected by the wait staff. Soft jazz music continued to play, alleviating Paul's tense feelings. It seemed, he ventured to believe, like an actual date: him and his old lady, enjoying their breakfast. A smile slowly crossed Paul's face.

"Would you like a refill?" Tracy inquired, returning to their table, and holding a pitcher of fresh orange juice.

"Sure," Paul said, less timidly.

After breakfast had been eaten and paid for, Paul was thankful that things went better than he had expected and that they were in an environment where nobody bothered them.

Maybe this place isn't so bad, Paul thought, warmth spreading throughout his chest. They both went back to Henry's vehicle and handed him his breakfast.

"What? A stupid cinnamon roll and orange juice?" Henry grumbled.

"You could have gone inside and had a real breakfast," Paul countered, smirking mischievously. He tried to suppress his laughter, knowing how much he had irritated his friend.

Henry shot Paul a cold look. Paul knew Henry despised eating cinnamon rolls. Mrs. Wilkerson used to make them often for breakfast, so frequently that Henry developed a distaste for them. Whenever Henry would be given a cinnamon roll for breakfast, he would wait until it was time to go to school and hurl it into the trashcan. Occasionally, some girls would flip their wigs and tell him that he was being wasteful, only for him to shout at them to mind their own business and that he was feeding the hungry ants. Currently, Henry must have been hungry because he began to devour the cinnamon roll, while muttering a few vulgarities under his breath.

"You got a container to put gas in?" Paul asked Henry.

"No," his friend answered, taking another bite of the cinnamon roll.

"I'm going to head up the road to the gas station," Paul said, tugging at his shirt. "They might have a container. I'll be back in a few minutes. Geeze, it's hot! You and Nell should go inside the restaurant where it's cooler. The people inside are friendly, so you don't have to worry about them."

"I already told you, I'm not going in."

"Then either go with me or go inside another building. It's your choice but stay nearby so we can be on our way once I get back."

"I'll just find another building to cool off in."

Paul faced Nell, who was seated in the backseat of the car. Opening the creaky door, he leaned forward, giving her shoulder a soft squeeze.

"I won't be gone long. Cool down inside the restaurant until I get back. I love you." Tilting forward, he gave Nell a quick smooch, before turning around and beginning his walk along the sidewalk. Wiping his sweaty brow with the back of his hand, Paul shut his eyes briefly, feeling the strong rays of sunlight hit his skin. He tugged at his clammy shirt that was starting to stick and shoved his hands into his pockets. Every so often, a tree would provide some shade from the scorching sun, easing the agonizing stroll. Luckily for him, he was used to his body enduring such stress from football practice. Paul began to imagine himself and the rest of the team doing their drills on the field, challenging each other, and making fun of their past blunders from previous games. Heck, he even recalled Coach Anderson bellowing at him to stay focused during games when he would easily become sidetracked with thoughts of girls, cars, or other matters.

Paul smirked at the recollections. Spotting a fallen pinecone on the ground, he picked it up. Imagining that it was a football, he threw it as far as he could down the road. Ordinarily, there would have been someone like Henry or another athlete that would have caught it, making a dash to score for the team, but there was nobody today, disheartening his spirit. Instead, the pinecone fell to the ground, moving off into the grass of a nearby ditch.

"Paul," a voice called out from behind him.

Turning around, Paul was surprised to see Nell hurrying to be with him. She, too, was sweaty with sticky clothes and her breathing was labored. Catching up to him, she bent forward, pressing the palms of her hands to her knees.

"Babe," Paul spoke, "What are you doing here? It's too hot for you to be walking this far. Go back to the restaurant and rest where it's cooler."

"I'd rather go with you than be stuck anywhere with Henry," Nell retorted, straightening up, and moving next to him. "A good walk never hurt anyone."

"Don't say I didn't warn you," Paul responded, recommencing the stroll.

"I didn't mean to eavesdrop, but I heard the conversation between you and Henry," Nell told him. "After what happened in our hometown, where do we stand? As Henry said, things would be easier for you without me. I want the truth. What do you want to do, as far as me and the baby goes?"

"We are as we were this morning, together," Paul answered. "Just because Henry and I are best friends doesn't mean that I'm going to always go by what he suggests or believes. Keep in mind, you and I knew the risks involved before we both decided to be together, and I stand by my decision. I love you, Nell. I regret nothing, other than not being careful enough with you to put you out of harm's way. I'm sorry for what happened. With any luck, I can make up for a lot of things. How about you? What are your thoughts?"

"I believe things will get better in some ways, like today. We can walk together without pretending we don't like each other."

"Also, neither of us has to worry about the math test for Mr. Thomas' class."

"Yeah, but we spent a lot of time studying for it. Thanks to you, I managed to get a low B in the class and was working to get my grade up to an A. If I were to the ace the test, I was going to surprise you."

"I'm still proud of you, Nell," said Paul. "I know you would have done well."

"How are we supposed to finish high school?" Nell wondered. "What about your scholarships? I'd hate for you to miss out on such wonderful opportunities. It's all my fault."

"Stop blaming yourself," Paul replied. "You have nothing to do with me missing anything. We can still finish high school; just not there. Remember this, no matter how much someone tries to take something away from you, there is always another way to succeed. It may not be our first choice nor the best, but there are still options for us."

"My parents are going to have a fit," Nell sighed. "They were eager for me to be the first in my family to graduate. Even with another way, they will be upset with me."

"You can still graduate; I know you can, and they will too."

When they arrived at the gas station, Paul used the remainder of his money to purchase a container and gas. The largest container the station had was a five-gallon metal container, not enough to fill the vehicle halfway. More money was needed, and they were completely out.

On the way back to the restaurant, Paul noticed the sign to a bank and trust company that was one of the many branches that held his funds: The Dupont Bank and Trust. It was the business owned and managed by his mother's side of the family, the Dupont twins, who assisted with his parents and grandfather's accounts throughout the years. Paul hardly spoke the twins since his grandfather's death, speaking to only one twin every Saturday with scarcely a few words between them. Though not members of "The Family," the twins were familiar with their practices and still conducted business with them, making Paul apprehensive at the thought of going into any of their establishments. The eldest twin, Simon, was the new trustee to his parents' estate. Previously, he had made a deal with Paul to continue his studies at his current school in Wood Oak. However, should Paul fail in any way, Simon promised that there would be severe consequences.

"I am so glad that you could join us for dinner, Simon," Paul's mother spoke gleefully, many years ago during a family gathering.

Ten-year-old Paul stared at the clean-cut man who hugged his mother. Simon Dupont was his mother's half-brother who was two years younger than she was. Simon and his identical twin brother, Seth, were thirty-seven years old. Paul couldn't tell either twin apart, but his mother amazingly could, telling him that Simon was the taller twin, not helping Paul distinguish either. Simon had hazel eyes and strawberry blonde hair that had a slight curl. He wore a solid black blazer, red and white tie, black pants, and polished black shoes. Unfortunately, so did Seth.

"And you Seth," Helen said hugging the other brother.

Simon and Seth lived in Camellia, Alabama and Helen always managed to keep close contact with both brothers, calling them every weekend.

"And you both remember Paul," Helen continued as all eyes fell upon the youth.

"Hello, Paul," the twins both spoke simultaneously, extending their hands.

Paul lingered near the doorway to the Dupont Bank and Trust building. *What did Uncle Simon mean by, should I fail, there would be severe consequences?* Paul certainly didn't want to find out. Ever since his mother's death, Simon's eyes and demeanor were more bitter than his grandfather, Abraham's and Paul could only imagine what would happen to him if he got on his uncle's bad side. Simon had more power, money, and connections.

"Grandfather," Paul said months ago, "What happened to Wally's father after what he did to my mother."

"When the twins saw your mother's condition," Abraham admitted, laying in the hospital bed, "they vowed to take revenge on Philip and if they couldn't get their justice, they would go after the other Boudreauxs in Wood Oak, including your father. When angry, the twins can be just as brutal as their father who was known to bury his enemies alive, leaving a small breathing hole. He would bury them deep in areas known to flood, forcing the person *to die of starvation or drowning. Philip's dying by my own hand was more merciful than anything the twins would have made him endure."*

The last time Paul had seen Simon, it was strictly business with no emotional attachment. He was treated no different than any other regular customer at the bank and trust. If Paul was given no preferential treatment, Simon could possibly have no qualms about torturing the youth just to make a point about failures.

Maybe I... could at least try, Paul thought. *Checking to see if I can take some money out shouldn't be any cause for alarm...But, if I took money out, Simon might question why I am taking out money here instead of my usual location, especially on a day I am expected to be in school. If people were upset about me dating Nell, I don't want to think about how Simon would react once he finds out about that too. If I take money out, it would have to be a ton before getting out of town, before he has a chance to find me.*

"Wait here for a little while, babe," Paul said, putting the gas container on the ground near Nell and entering the building. When it was time for Paul to speak to the teller, of course, Paul asked if Simon would be aware of the transaction. The teller confirmed that Simon would be notified of each transaction. All Paul could do was exhale and leave the building, without making any withdrawals.

"Were you able to get what you need?" Nell asked Paul, who picked up the container.

"No," said Paul, recommencing the walk between them. He wished that he had his own vehicle. He always had spare funds in the glove compartment and *his* car's gas gage was never broken.

Paul was getting irritated, especially since a mosquito began buzzing near his ear. He quickened his pace, but the bothersome buzzing persisted. Paul bent his ear near his shoulder, until he placed the gas container on the ground and began swatting at the annoying pest. The mosquito landed on his arm, only for Paul to smack and kill it. He brushed it off, lifted the container once more, and headed back to the restaurant parking lot.

Chapter 3

Upon arrival at the parking lot, Paul wasn't surprised to see that Henry had decided to split, leaving his vehicle with the doors locked. Paul scanned the lot with his eyes searching for his friend, but Henry was nowhere in sight. Opening the gas cap to the car, Paul asked Nell to go back into the restaurant to see if Henry was inside, but when she returned, she verbalized that nobody had seen Henry.

"Henry bugs me sometimes, you know that," Paul informed Nell. "He could have at least left a note telling us where he was going to be. Let me finish refueling the car, so I can go and search for him. As hot as it is outside, you'd think he'd have some sense to get over himself and go inside the restaurant. I'll check the other businesses."

Paul poured the last of the fuel into the tank. He instructed for Nell to go back inside the restaurant, while he searched for Henry. Placing the empty gas container down next to the car, Paul went next door to an old bakery and asked if they had seen the missing teen. Sadly, none of the employees nor customers knew of Henry's whereabouts. Paul went to six other businesses who also didn't see the youth. Henry had vanished without a trace. Hunting for more clues near the original restaurant, Paul went towards the back of Leroy's. There were a few cardboard boxes and trash bags sticking out the nearly filled dumpster. Paul spotted a narrow opening between two wood boards on a fence. His heartbeat increasing with each step closer. Flies dancing around him; Paul pushed his way between the fence, seeing wildflowers, a improvised chicken coop, and a medium sized vegetable garden in the backyard of an old wooden shotgun house that had been painted pink. Yards away from the house was a tall pecan tree and inches away from the tree was the body of Paul's friend, Henry. A heavy feeling in his stomach, Paul rushed his way, turning him over onto his back. Henry was heavily sweating, and his skin was clammy.

"Henry," Paul yelled, his voice elevating, "Are you okay? What happened?" He began to call out for help, examining the area. Henry let out a low, soft groan. He had no wounds, cuts, nor blood on him, but he was weak.

"It's so hot," Henry murmured, his voice barely audible. Dragging Henry closer the shade created by the pecan tree, Paul continued to call out for help, hoping that someone would come to his aid.

Then, the backdoor to the shotgun house opened, revealing an elderly Negro woman, who was in her late seventies. Her grey hair was covered with a white cloth, and she wore a long, worn brown dress. Her face was covered with wrinkles and her faded brown eyes fell upon the two young men.

"My friend needs help," Paul called out to her. "I think he's overheated!"

"Bring him inside," the elderly woman told him, widening the access to her house.

Pulling one of Henry's arms over his shoulder, Paul dragged his friend to the inside of the woman's home. Inside the backroom, there was a single-sized bed that Paul laid Henry on. Thankfully, the room had an air conditioner that was on, cooling it. The room also had an old, worn upholstered chair, dresser, and closet.

The elderly woman left the room briefly, returning with a tall glass of water and a damp cloth. Right away, Paul aided in removing Henry's shirt and began to press the cold, damp cloth against Henry's skin that was handed to him. Then, he began to bring the glass of water up to Henry's lips, only for it to run down his chin. Henry began to cough, forcing Paul to slow down his efforts in rehydrating his friend. The woman grabbed a hand fan from the dresser and began to fan Henry.

"Yep, heat exhaustion," the woman spoke. "Give him some time to recover."

Henry pressed the palm of his hands against his forehead, leaning down on top of the pillow of the bed.

"Are you feeling better?" Paul questioned him.

"Yeah," Henry said closing his eyes again.

Paul studied the room further. The walls were wooden and had pictures on the dresser. A second door from the room led to another room that looked like it was bigger with more furnishings.

His mind racing, Paul speculated, *how were they to recover should another incident occur?* The gas tank to the car wasn't filled enough to make it to the middle Florida. What could they do with so little resources? It was almost maddening with all the troubles that were beginning to grow worse by the hour. Paul was sweaty, sticky, and disgusted. Watching Henry lay down in the bed made Paul wish he were back at home, in his own bed, resting and refreshed. It had been an exhausting day and he was tired of all the complications. Everything was becoming overwhelming, beyond his control. Paul's shoulders dropped and his chest began to cave in.

"Would you like some water too?" the woman asked him.

Paul nodded and waited. He covered his eyes with his hands and let out a low muffled groan. Then, removing his hands, Paul gazed up and saw the elderly woman standing near him with another tall glass of water in her hands. He clutched the glass and brought it to his lips, guzzling it down.

"Thank you," he said, pressing his hand against his head. He fought back the lightheadedness. The woman left the room once more, leaving Paul alone with Henry. Paul turned again towards the dresser. He glanced at the pictures of the smiling faces, unexpectedly realizing that one of the pictures was that of a man that seemed familiar. The man was a middle-aged Negro man with black hair, brown eyes, and a handsome smile. It was the man that his uncle, Harry Boudreaux, had murdered years ago.

Chapter 4

Paul's eyes widened momentarily when the elderly woman returned to the room. *In what way did she know the man in the picture?* Paul recalled the man as the same Negro man who often visited his Aunt Henrietta while the rest of the family was away. Paul was thirteen at the time and living with his grandfather. He never spoke of the things he would see when he would look outside the window, seeing the man leave the home many times just before his abusive uncle and cousins would return home from Sal's Country Store. Paul remembered the day the man was shot and his aunt shouting that he had raped her, knowing that it was all a lie.

There was a tightness in Paul's chest, at the realization. *How could he even address the kind woman, knowing someone in his family took the life of someone she knew?*

"That's a picture of my son, Otis Griffin," the woman said, taking notice of Paul's brief stare and lifting the picture from the dresser. "I look at his picture, every day, to see him. He used to be enlisted as a radio operator in the Air Force for four years before coming back home to Louisiana to work at the post office. He moved to Wood Oak where he said he had reconnected with an old girlfriend, saying that no matter how long it took, he was going to marry her. I was amazed that he still found the time to visit me, as busy as he was. I miss his visits...I'd always greet him and tell him to 'give me some sugar' and kiss his cheek, as I've always done since he was a child. Things were fine until one day he stopped coming. Turned out that he had been killed by a white man who said that my son, the man that I raised, raped his wife in the middle of a robbery. Can you believe that? Not even to this day have I ever believed such a vicious accusation. My son would never do such horrible things."

Paul took a deep, pained breath. The story was not shocking for him, for he, too, knew that the accusation was a lie and part of a cruel cycle that had gone on for far too long in his family. The brutalities and the coverups needed to stop. Paul's head hung low, ashamed. *Hopefully, it will come to an end, with me.*

"I'm sorry," Paul spoke, his voice dismayed, "for what happened to your son. I hope that one day, he will get the justice that he deserves." *I wish that there were more that I could do. Uncle Harry deserves the worst fate imaginable and Aunt Henrietta...how could she had been so selfish? I don't know how long it will take or when I will ever get ahold of the right person to pull the proper strings, but I will find a way! Otis isn't the first person to have lost his life at the hands of my family.*

"What are your names?" the woman asked, "I've never seen you two around here before."

"I'm Paul and he is Henry," Paul spoke, daring to not say his last name nor where they were from. "We are from out of town. We were on our way to Florida when we ran into a bit of trouble, as you can see."

"You aren't running from the law, are you?"

"No, ma'am. What is your name?"

Henry's breathing had normalized, and his eyes were open, listening to the conversation.

"You can call me Mrs. Ann," said the elderly woman.

"Thank you for helping us, Mrs. Ann," Paul said. "We will be out shortly."

"No rush," Mrs. Ann stated. "I was in the middle of doing some laundry when I heard you calling for help outside. I do folks' laundry and iron clothes to earn a few dollars here and there. In an hour, I'm going to start prepping for lunch. You and your friend are welcomed to stay and eat before heading to Florida."

"That's very kind of you," Paul responded, "but, if you don't mind, there would be one more person joining: my girlfriend, Nell. She would love to meet you."

"Sure, she can join us," said Mrs. Ann. "My niece, Tracy, works at the restaurant behind the house called Leroy's. My brother owns it, and Tracy comes here occasionally to check up on me during her break."

"Leroy's," Paul repeated. "My old lady and I had a great breakfast there this morning! Tracy was our waitress!"

"Yep, that's her," replied Mrs. Ann. "I'm going to finish working on the laundry. The food should be ready by twelve." With that, she walked into another room, deep within the house.

Henry lifted his head from the pillow and began rapping his fingers against his thigh, staring at back door. Paul knew what that meant: Henry didn't want to be there. His outspoken friend was unusually quiet and anytime Henry was silent, something was amiss. They both rose to their feet and exited the home from the backdoor. The tension was intense and when they both reached the fence, Henry began moving towards his automobile. As much as Paul didn't want to be bothered with more problems, he broke his silence.

"You going back to Mrs. Ann's place for lunch?" he questioned his friend, already knowing the answer.

"Do you even have to ask?" Henry stated, sardonically.

"You know what, what's with you?" Paul demanded. "If it wasn't for her, you would still be laying on the ground from heat exhaustion. Can't you be grateful?"

"Then let me stay on the ground next time," Henry shot back. "I don't owe that old battle axe anything. I could have made it to the shade underneath that pecan tree on my own. I was only resting my eyes for a little bit. Just because you're seeing Nell doesn't mean you have to be friendly with all the coloreds you run into. Let's get out of here. The sooner we leave, the better."

"And where to? We don't have any more money, the gas tank isn't full, and there is no way we can make it to the middle of Florida!"

"Blame Nell for that, not me."

"You're starting to bug me again," Paul exclaimed. "Stop blaming her! I'm tired of hearing it! In case you forgot, it wasn't her who forced us to leave town."

"If people like *her* would have stayed at their own school, none of this would have happened! Everything was fine until they came. We both could have been hanging out with the guys, making out with hot broads, or betting at the racetrack! Instead, we are running around like a bunch of fugitives in the middle of nowhere!"

"Where did you expect the colored students to go when their school burned down?"

"Anywhere but Wood Oak High School! I don't care where *they* would have gone, just keep out of *ours*! 'The white man this, the white man that!' All the coloreds do is sit around and mope about how they are suffering, just like that old hag in the house back there. Everyone loses someone! Yet, again, we, white men, get blamed for *everything*! I'm sick of it! I'm not going back there to listen to another round of passing the blame onto us!"

"Unbelievable," Paul groaned. "You know what, maybe you *should have* stayed on the ground! We both know that there are racial problems everywhere and that both of our families had done some awful things based on race alone. Have you even considered to think that what she said is true and that her son's murderer just so happens to be white? Everyone knows colored men get it bad if they mess with white women. I would know, my family are some of the guiltiest out there! The point of the matter is that her son didn't get justice because he was colored. Think about it, regardless of the situation, did he deserve to lose his life?"

"Maybe he did," Henry countered. "What was he doing there in the first place? If he didn't want to be shot, he shouldn't have been where he wasn't supposed to be. Learn from him and stay in your own lane too. You would have been a dead man yourself if it weren't for me. You're welcome, from a *white* guy who saved your life, not some colored!"

"Ha! All the times *I* vouched for *your* family. That's the least you could do. Whether you choose to go or not, Nell and I will be having lunch at Mrs. Ann's house. I appreciate you helping us out at Wood Oak, but all this hatred you have towards Nell and all colored people needs to stop. I'm going back inside the restaurant to check on her. I already filled your car's gas tank with some gas. It's not enough to get to the middle of Florida, but I put in everything I had."

With that, Paul moved past Henry and reentered the restaurant. Ignoring the prying eyes of a few patrons, he checked the dining room, seeking Nell. She was seated at a table in the far back of the restaurant with a glass of water in front of her, talking to Tracy, who casually sat across from her at the table. Both were laughing over some mysterious joke between them. Noticing Paul, Nell waved him over to the table just as Tracy left to attend to another customer.

"Were you able to find Henry?" Nell asked.

"Yes," Paul said, "I found him passed out from heat exhaustion behind the restaurant in a lady's backyard. He's probably back at the car; you know how stubborn he is."

"How are you two friends? He is so disrespectful to people!"

"He most definitely is, but he's not too terrible once he gets to know someone."

"I don't want to get to know someone like him or vice versa."

"If that's the case, you two might get along because that sounds like something he would say."

Returning to the table, Tracy refilled Nell's glass of water.

"You must have loved the food to be returning so soon," Tracy told Paul. "Would you like something to drink?"

"No, thanks," Paul responded. "I met your aunt, Mrs. Ann who lives in the house in the back of the restaurant. She was kind enough to invite us to have lunch at her house."

"Sounds like she is taking away some of our customers," Tracy said, smirking. "But it's good that she has company. My aunt doesn't get too many visitors outside of me and my dad at her house. Other than us, she stays busy doing laundry for the folks that she works for. Most of her friends had passed away. I think she gets lonely in that house; I certainly would! That's why I visit her from time to time. Well, I better tend to these other folks."

Leaving the table, Tracy began to tend to the other customers.

"You ready to go?" Paul asked Nell.

"Sure," she said following him outside the establishment.

Sulking, Paul took notice that not only was Henry gone, but his car as well. He prayed that Nell wouldn't have also taken notice. There was nothing else to do and he had no money nor ideas to distract her, until one hit him. *Maybe we could go back to Mrs. Ann's since Tracy did say that she was lonely. It's still early and she could probably use the help or company.*

"Let me introduce you to Mrs. Ann," Paul said taking Nell to the back of the restaurant towards Mrs. Ann's house. "So, how did things go while I was gone?"

"Not much happened," said Nell. "I went back inside the restaurant and asked to use the phone. They let me, even though I told them it would be a long-distance call to my parents, but when I called home, nobody answered. I got water and talked to Tracy for a little bit between her customers. She asked who you were to me and was stunned to hear that we were together."

Paul squeezed between the fence and Nell followed him into the backyard.

"She also said you were very good looking," Nell added, a hint of animosity in her voice.

Paul couldn't help but snicker at the disclosure. He didn't dare to look at Nell, but the mere thought of her being jealous over him boosted his ego.

"And what did *you* say?" Paul asked, his senses heightening.

"I said you looked okay," Nell responded, making Paul stop in his tracks. He shot her an irritated glance, making Nell grin.

"Just okay? C'mon! How could you say something like that?"

"I was kidding, Paul!"

"Then what did you say?"

"I agreed that you were good looking, okay!"

Paul stopped by the pecan tree, resting against it.

"Good looking, huh?" he said, motioning for her to get closer. With Nell closer, he pressed his lips against hers. "And I think you're beautiful, babe." He smirked as the jolt of electricity spread at the touch of Nell wrapping her arms around him.

"You're such a romantic, Paul Boudreaux," Nell giggled.

"I can't help it, you have that effect on me," Paul whispered, giving her another kiss. "I love you, baby."

"I love you too."

Beaming, they both began to walk again. Reaching down, Paul put Nell's hand in his. He gave it a slight, cheerful swing, eventually brining it up to his lips and kissing it. From the corner of his eye, he saw Nell's smile broaden, bringing a radiating warmth throughout his body.

"Paul," Nell said, stopping their walk, "since we are no longer in Wood Oak and don't need to hide our feelings towards each other anymore, would it be okay if I took your school ring out?"

"Sure," Paul agreed, watching Nell remove the hidden school ring from underneath her outfit as it hanged from her golden necklace. Now everyone would know that they were officially going steady together. "Babe, I left a lot of things back home, but there was one item I always carry with me and I'm glad that I still have it." Paul reached into his pants pocket and pulled out the handmade handkerchief that Nell had given to him months ago. "I'd never leave my handkerchief behind, ever."

They proceeded to continue their stroll together to the house. Paul knocked on the backdoor before turning the handle to open the door.

"Mrs. Ann," Paul called out, "It's Paul. I'm back with my girlfriend, Nell. We're in the backroom."

"I'll be there in a minute," Mrs. Ann's voice responded from a distance.

Paul stood while Nell sat down on the upholstered chair. Moments later, Mrs. Ann reemerged into the room doing a double take at the sight of Nell.

"Mrs. Ann, this is my girlfriend, Nell," Paul said, beaming.

"Nice to meet you, Nell," Mrs. Ann greeted Nell.

"Nice meeting you too," Nell responded.

"Make yourselves comfortable," Mrs. Ann stated. "I'm just finishing the laundry and will be getting lunch prepped in a few minutes. We are going to be having some catfish, corn bread, okra, and peach cobbler."

"Wow, that sounds great," Nell exclaimed, her voice almost squealing. "Earlier, I told Paul that I had a craving for catfish! Would you like for us to help you prepare the food? That way we can earn our keep."

"Sure," Ann agreed. "That would be helpful. Where's 'Red' at? Isn't he going to join us?"

Paul rubbed the back of his neck, unable to meet Mrs. Ann's questionable eyes. There was no way that he could respond to her question without giving a hurtful answer, especially if he wanted to be candid. Heck! Paul didn't even know himself where Henry went off to this time, but one thing was for certain, Paul knew that Henry would eventually get hungry, wherever he was. *Oh well, his loss!*

"He's busy with the car," Paul responded.

"Doesn't sound like any of you will be making it to Florida today," said Mrs. Ann. "You got a place to stay in town? There are a few affordable hotels nearby."

"Thanks, but we can stay in Henry's car," Paul stated, hesitantly, almost cringing at the very statement himself. "We can't afford to stay in a hotel. We spent the last of our money getting gas."

"*Staying in a car*?" Mrs. Ann cried out. "No, sir! I can help with that. If y'all need money and aren't in a rush to get to your destination, I can talk to my brother about having Nell help out at the restaurant. For you, I know this white auto mechanic named Mr. Holiday. I usually collect and do laundry for him and a few other folks once a week. He owns a garage several blocks away from here. He gets along with everybody and rents out the rooms of his house every now and then, but Nell must stay here. While most Negroes and whites tolerate each other in this neck of the woods, they don't house together in this town; that's just the way it is. Mr. Holiday has some prejudiced neighbors and if they ever found out that he was boarding a Negro girl in his house, they would have a fit. You can talk to Mr. Holiday and work out a deal with him. He is willing to hire men who are good with cars. You do know something about cars, don't you? When Tracy stops by, I can get her to drive you to Mr. Holiday's business."

Paul's heart sank. *Separated from Nell? Again! After everything we've been through?* Mrs. Ann seemed to be a nice lady, but he wasn't sure if he wanted to trust leaving Nell to someone he had only known for a few minutes, but without many options, he had no choice but to comply. Afterall, Mrs. Ann knew Magnolia better than he did.

A few hours later, after lunch, Tracy showed up at Mrs. Ann's house. After speaking with her aunt, she drove Nell and Paul to a street that was thirty blocks away from Mrs. Ann's house.

The street had additional trees and businesses ranging from trendy clothing stores to popular fast-food chains. Tracy parked her car in front of a red building that had a white sign that read, "Holiday's Garage." The garage consisted of four bays being used by four white mechanics who were busily operating on different automobiles. On the side of each bay were industrial fans, toolboxes, floor jacks, and metallic trashcans. Against the back wall were racks filled with oil filters, air filters, and a variety of different tires. Next to the bay to the far right of the building was the waiting room that had a single door entrance in the front and a second entrance that separated the building from the bay area. Furthermore, the structure had tall glass panels that had hand painted advertisements for shop deals such as oil changes, tune ups, and other works offered by the business.

"Mr. Holiday is the short, elderly man," Tracy informed Paul, pointing to a balding elderly man in his late sixties dressed in grey coveralls, in the first bay, near the waiting room. "Just wait for him in the waiting area and speak to him about needing work and a place to stay. Mr. Holiday is nice, but he won't just hire anybody to work in his shop. When it comes to him, your first impression is the *only* impression, so you must know your stuff when it comes to cars. You know anything about cars, don't cha?"

"Sure," said Paul, his voice confident.

"Alright, good luck," Tracy replied.

"Thanks for telling me," Paul said. He turned to Nell, who squeezed his hand. Her eyes were saddened, knowing that this was another farewell.

"Don't worry," Tracy assured them. "Nell can stay with my aunt, and she can help around the restaurant. She'll be alright. You'll enjoy working for Mr. Holiday. That is, if he chooses to give you a job. If not, call me at this number; I'll pick you up and we can think of something else." She handed him a piece of paper that had a telephone number on it. Paul tucked the paper into his pants pocket.

Thank goodness I paid attention in Mr. Payne's class, Paul thought. This should be easy if he is as fair as Tracy and Mrs. Ann says he is. I need this job!

It was time to go.

Embracing Nell, Paul spoke, "after I get the job, I'll come by and visit as often as I can; I promise." He leaned forward, kissing her. "I love you, babe."

"I love you too, Paul," Nell said, returning the kiss.

Paul withdrew from the car. He watched Tracy drive Nell away, taking the same route they had entered. Paul stood there, alone, in front of the shop. Taking a deep breath, he strode to the entrance of the building and opened the door to the waiting room. Inside the building were three people, a young mother and her two young children, one around the age of three and the other at least five years old. The children were running about the lobby, with their mother ordering them to sit back down and be quiet. The children reminded Paul of the Wilkersons. All the running around and driving their parents up the wall was something Henry regularly complained about, often leading him to leaving the household and going on his wild drives around town as a means of escape.

Paul sat down in a chair across from the young family and before he knew it, Mr. Holiday entered the waiting room, calling the woman towards him. He and the young mother spoke, and she handed him money from her purse. She soon left the building with her children, appearing as exhausted as she did when Paul first entered the facility.

Mr. Holiday beckoned Paul over to him. With a steady gait and wide steps, Paul approached the elder.

"What kind of car repairs are you needing today, son?" Mr. Holiday questioned him. "We have a good deal on tires, if you're needing that."

"Thanks; but not today," answered Paul. "I'm actually here for a job…and a place to board."

"How much you got on you?" Mr. Holiday asked him.

"Nothing."

Mr. Holiday shot him a skeptical look before saying, "I guess you could earn your board. Do you know anything about cars?"

"Yes, sir. I used to take an auto shop class at my old high school. I know how to change tires, check and do oil changes, check tire air pressures, and other things."

"Is that so," Mr. Holiday said folding his arms across his chest. "What's your name?"

"Paul Boudreaux."

"Tell me, Paul, how you would change the oil to a car?"

"Jack up the car and lift the car with a jack stand. Put an oil drain pan underneath. You open the drain plug.

Let the oil drain out. Remove the filter and replace it with a new one. Then pour in the new oil, depending on how much is needed."

Mr. Holiday nodded, unfolding his arms.

"Sounds like you do know a few things," he said. "How old are you?"

"Seventeen."

"You finished school?"

"I'm not in school anymore. I am just seeking work and a place to stay."

"You can work around the shop in exchange for your lodging. I'll throw in a few dollars because a man has to eat. Pay day is every Friday, at the beginning of your shift. I pay cash. I'll introduce you to the other mechanics and you can start out cleaning around the garage, checking the oil to the cars, washing the windshields, and checking the tire air pressures. After work, which is at 6 p.m., I can show you where the house is. Where's your vehicle and belongings?"

"I don't have either."

"For heaven's sake, son! Don't you have anything?"

Chapter 5

It was the next morning. Mr. Holiday lived in a four-bedroom house in an upper middle-class neighborhood. The area was lovely with oak trees, mowed lawns, and flower gardens, reminding Paul of the middle-class neighborhood that his former girlfriend, Nancy Perkins, lived in.

Mr. Holiday began the day with a tall cup of hot coffee that he poured into a grey metallic thermos, taking a few sips before closing it with a lid. His breakfast consisted of nothing more than a simple piece of toast with a single spread of butter. A second piece of toast was given to Paul for his breakfast, with the addition of a small glass of water.

"I don't do any cooking," Mr. Holiday admitted. "I mainly eat out at the diner across the street for lunch and eat lunchmeat sandwiches for dinner, but you can feel free to use anything that's in the kitchen. There's a few more slices of bread on the counter, a few bits of meat and cheese in the refrigerator. You're welcome to any of it, but don't be wasteful. My boarders usually either eat out or cook their own meals on the gas stove with the groceries they buy for themselves."

Paul grimaced. He didn't cook either! Oh well, at least he had a chance to eat a good meal the day before at Leroy's restaurant and Mrs. Ann's house. Today, a sandwich would be fine; it was better than nothing and he wasn't picky when it came to eating meats and breads. He was grateful to have anything at all and a roof over his head. Paul began to chew on his toast, savoring the buttery taste.

"Since you don't have much, I can buy you lunch at the diner today," Mr. Holiday offered. "Don't worry about paying it back. I'll just consider it as my good deed for the day."

"Thank you," Paul said, finishing the toast.

"It's no problem," Mr. Holiday stated. "You're going to like eating at Tilly's Diner. They have some of the best jambalaya and boudin in town. If you're more of a red beans and rice kind of guy, they have that too, but if you get as gassy as Luke, don't bother!"

Paul had a small room that had wooden walls and a single bed to the east side of the home. It had a single window that had blinds and brown curtains. There was a closet and a dresser. The room was a great contrast to his old room that used to have books, magazines, a color television set, and more things to entertain himself.

The kitchen to the home had a basic refrigerator, gas stove, and oven. A few clean dishes were neatly stacked on top of each other near the sink. The living room had a tiny black and white television, an old, recycled couch, a bookshelf with various books, and a sofa. The other rooms were just as baren as Paul's, except for the room that Mr. Holiday occupied himself. His room consisted of a single bed, a closet full of clothes, stacks of newspapers and car magazines piled high, random pictures of unknown individuals, and other various belongings, crowding the room. There was a single uncluttered path leading from the entrance of the room to his bed.

Mr. Holiday had extra clothes that former boarders had left behind that Paul was welcomed to for a change of clothes. Usually when tenants left clothes behind, Mr. Holiday would have Mrs. Ann clean them so that he could donate them to the local thrift store. Luckily for Paul, Mr. Holiday had not given the clothes to the thrift store that week, leaving him clothes to choose from that had already been washed, ironed, and folded. Paul picked out the most fitting and comfortable clothes, only to have the shirt and pants be covered up by his grey work coveralls.

With a long workday ahead of them, Paul joined Mr. Holiday into his green truck. The rusty door creaked when it opened and closed, signaling for a neighbor to greet the duo with a brief smile and wave as they made their way down the street to the garage. Upon arrival to their destination, the other three mechanics had already gathered near the building, engaged in conversation about cars, politics, protests, and the Vietnam war.

Withdrawing from the truck, Mr. Holiday reintroduced Paul to the mechanics: Luke Scott, an eighteen-year-old, brown haired and brown eyed youth; Matthew Smith, a twenty-seven-year-old man with black hair and green eyes; Aaron Blake, a blonde-haired, blue-eyed man in his mid-thirties. All were dressed in grey coveralls that had their names and the name of the shop sewn on the top right section of their outfits.

As ordered, Paul began the day cleaning around the waiting area and helping in parts of the bay. Mr. Holiday showed Paul how to do inventory and what to do when the tire truck pulled in for unloading. He sorted out the tires, stacking them into a visually appealing display, reminding him of his former duties back at Sal's Country Store. It was a long, busy day for everyone, and more cars began to fill the parking lot with hopes of getting timely repairs.

Sccccrrreeeeccchhhh! Vvvvrrrrrroooooommmm!

Making a sharp, lethal turn, a recognizable car swerved into the parking lot, barely avoiding hitting a parked car in front of the building. Flabbergasted, Paul, the mechanics, and a few bystanders gawked at Henry, who stormed from the automobile, pointing a finger at Paul.

"You and me, in the car," Henry ordered.

Befuddled, Paul's head flinched back slightly. His eyebrows squished together while he continued to stand in place, frozen. *What is Henry trying to do? Fight me out in the parking lot? The last time we got into a brawl with each other was back in elementary school over something foolish that I can't even remember. Now, after all this time, he wants to quarrel because I didn't want to leave Nell. Sometimes, he can be such an idiot, arguing over things that don't matter. I'd expect something like this from Bill, but not him.*

Paul blew out his cheeks and released the air between his lips.

The mechanics began to gather near Paul.

"Whose that bozo?" Aaron asked.

"Is he looking for a fight," Luke questioned Paul. "Because if he is, we can all take him."

"It's okay," Paul answered, moving towards Henry who was leaning against the side of his car with his arms folded across his chest. Henry's stance didn't indicate that he had any intensions to attack Paul, but his eyes were dull, and his lips were tightly pressed together. Usually during this time, Henry would have been smelling of smoke, but without money, even he was compelled to quit his bad habit temporarily, making him more on edge.

"Sorry about the other day, but I needed to cool off," Henry told Paul when they both entered the automobile. "I drove around until I found a store that had a parking lot that had tons of trees. I took a nap, but by the time I woke up, it was nighttime. So, I stayed where I was until this morning. I found a phone booth and had to dig deep between the seat cushions to find some spare change to make the call. I have some terrible news. *None of us can ever go back to Wood Oak. 'The Family' told my folks that they had three days to skip town and they were still packing when I called. Nell's family had less time. They had to leave the same day we left. Your cousin, Wally, didn't waste any time moving into your grandfather's old house. Talk about being an opportunist... I can't stand people like him."*

Paul touched his temple while he closed his eyes. He let out an uncontrollable groan. *What do you mean? Moving into my grandfather's place? I have barely been gone for a day and already Wally is trying to steal everything I own! I thought that there might have been the tiniest bit of a chance that after some time, I could go back, but, getting rid of me and anyone who allied with me...Wow, Wally, you're just as much of a monster as Uncle Harry. I was such a fool for trying so hard to give any of you a chance.*

So many emotions and thoughts were hitting Paul at once. *I did everything I could possibly do to share what I had, even offering to give them things that Grandfather told me not to give them and still that wasn't enough! I'm such a chump! I wouldn't blame Nell nor Henry if they just went their separate ways, away from me.*

"I should speak to your folks," Paul said, his voice breaking. "I didn't think things would go this far and involve your families getting kicked out of Wood Oak too."

"Not a good idea," Henry replied. "It would be best to wait until things have calmed down a bit. They are in disbelief and fuming about having to move at the last minute."

"What does your family plan to do?" Paul asked.

"They plan on going to my great aunt's place until they can figure something out," sighed Henry. "I already know that Aunt Agnes isn't going to like any of this. I can already see my folks and the old hag screaming at me to control the younger kids. I'm not dealing with it! I'd rather stay here than deal with all of them, but everyone is expecting for us to be there. Well, you and me. I didn't mention Nell for obvious reasons."

"Seems like Nell and I are better off here than in Florida," Paul uttered. "If she can't go, I won't go."

"What?" Henry squabbled. "There's nothing here for us! At least in Florida we will have food and a roof over our heads. You keep giving up too much to be with Nell."

"My new boss offered to let me stay with him," Paul informed Henry. "I'm exchanging work for a place to stay and a few dollars. Nell is doing the same with working back at the restaurant and is staying at Mrs. Ann's place. It's a start. How'd you even find out where I was?"

"I drove back to where Mrs. Ann lived and asked where you were," Henry responded. "She said you would be here, and I was hoping to pick you up so we could be on our way."

"Not a chance, but you're free to go to Florida if you want."

"You know I don't have enough gas or money to get to the middle of Florida!" Henry's face scrunched with tension in his voice.

"Sounds like you can't leave Magnolia either," Paul said nonchalantly, shrugging his shoulders half-heartedly, "unless you can get your folks to send you some money or pick you up. I don't have any more money either, remember!"

"They don't have any money to give me! They had to pawn everything they have just to get money to go to Florida themselves! What do you mean pick me up? I'm not leaving my car here!"

"See, another reason on why you should stay. Unlike them, you have nothing to pawn but your rifle and possibly your car, but that would leave you hitchhiking throughout Florida or them picking you up along the way."

"Riding with all of them is not an option for me. I'm not dealing with all those kids bickering at once! My nerves are too bad to deal with all that crap! What do you mean you don't have any money? You're loaded, why can't you just take some money out of your bank account and let me pay you back?"

"I can't simply withdraw money from my account. You know how messed up my family is! Do you really want them to find out that we are stranded in Magnolia like sitting ducks so they can finish the job of killing us?"

There was a tap on the car window. There stood Mr. Holiday, seething. Swiftly, Paul departed from the car.

"Sorry," Paul spoke. "There was an emergency, and my friend was here to tell me."

"An emergency, you say," Mr. Holiday said, wrinkling his brow. "Anything I can do to help?"

"Well," Paul began, his voice trailing.

Chapter 6

Slowly the headlights of a car grazed the outside exterior of the shotgun house that Tuesday evening. The sun was setting, and the neighborhood children were beginning to head inside to eat the dinners prepared by their mothers. Soon, the streetlights would begin to shine, bringing small, guided lights to the streets. The car stopped in front of Mrs. Ann's house and its passenger climbed out of the vehicle. Approaching the front door, the figure lifted his hand, giving the door a firm knock.

Opening the door, Nell glanced onto the figure in front of her. Instantly her eyes lit up when Paul wrapped his arms around her. They lingered before Paul tilted his head, playfully kissing Nell's neck. Giggling, Nell tilted her head, giving him a deepened kiss.

"Paul," Nell said cheerfully, "I didn't expect to see you so soon. How'd you get here? You didn't walk all this way, did you?"

"Henry came back, and I borrowed his car for tonight," said Paul. "He owed me for convincing Mr. Holiday to also hire him and give him a place to stay. You want to go out and have some fun?"

"I've been on my feet all day, but sure, as long as I don't have to do a lot of standing."

Closing the door behind them, Nell followed Paul back to Henry's car. He opened the front passenger side door for her before going back to the other side to sit in the driver's seat. Paul had no idea where they would be driving off to; everything would be spontaneous, yet exciting as far as he was concerned.

Shortly, they came across a park that had a field where several teens were hanging out, dancing to music blasting from car radios, making out, or playing baseball. The batter swung his wooden bat, hitting the ball. The ball flew towards the end of the field as the batter ran to first base and a player from the opposing team rushed to catch the ball that fell and rolled on the ground away from him.

Paul parked near the fence. Nell slid closer and Paul wrapped his arm around her, watching the game. Not too far from them, in the stands, two young kids around seven or eight years old were arguing over a chocolate candy bar, making Paul wonder if Nell, too, was hungry. She hadn't said anything to him, and he hoped that she wasn't holding back any type of hunger from him. Paul hadn't gotten paid yet, but if he had to, he could always make a deal with a small eatery, as he did with Mr. Holiday, if they were willing.

"Did you eat already?" Paul inquired.

"Too much," Nell laughed. "Mrs. Ann likes to cook, and she made some smothered chicken, rice, green beans, and apple pie. She kept offering me seconds, but trust me, one plate of her food is more than enough even when eating for two. How about you?"

"I had the *best* ham and cheese sandwich you could think of," Paul chuckled. "Where I'm at, none of us can cook. It's okay; I can't complain. It's food. Mr. Holiday took me and Henry to this diner called Tilly's for lunch. They make a pretty good jambalaya and gumbo."

"We have some men in the kitchen at Leroy's, and they are amazing cooks," Nell informed him. "They make the best macaroni and cheese using evaporated milk! It's so good! Anyway, how are things going for you at the garage? Is Mr. Holiday nice to you?"

"Since it was my first day, it was pretty much light duty work," Paul said. "Just sweeping, checking inventory; nothing too big. I could do more, but since I'm still seventeen, Mr. Holiday won't let me handle the other cars yet. Oh yeah, when Henry showed up, he was also put on light duty. He also told me some bad news. When we left Wood Oak, his family and your family were also forced to leave. Would you happen to know where they could have possible gone off to on such short notice?"

"My family is pretty small," Nell said taking a deep breath. "But the only people I can think of that would know for sure would be my Uncle Harold and Aunt Shirley who live in Illinois or Uncle Walter who lives in Michigan. The only problem is, I don't have the address book that has their addresses or phone numbers. My mother used to keep that information in a small, brown, address booklet."

"I'll check on that."

"What about you, Paul? Don't you have any other family to go to that aren't like the ones in Wood Oak?"

"The only other family I have left would be my mother's twin brothers from Alabama. Simon is my trustee, but both twins hate my father's side of the family. Both sides only tolerated each other this long was because of me, but I don't trust either."

"If your mother's side hates those prejudiced people on your father's side, they sound like a better option to go to."

"They doesn't hate my father's side because they're prejudiced; the twins hates them because of what my father's brother did to my mother years ago before I was born. It's some pretty heavy stuff to talk about."

"Would they be against us being together?"

"It's hard to say. I've never known them to openly say anything against anyone, but I barely communicate with them at all. All I can go by is what I've heard from my grandfather, but maybe he was just being biased. I've only seen Simon twice since my grandfather's death and it's only been at my mother's gravesite. Other than that, I've been giving him weekly calls telling him that things are fine at school and at home. That's it. Technically, after my grandfather passed, Simon is my new guardian until I turn eighteen. I was only allowed to stay in Wood Oak because I had to beg him to stay to finish out my school year. He agreed as long as I continued to go to school, finish, and call him every weekend. He and Mr. Wilkerson had an agreement to supervise me while I remained in Louisiana, but if Simon finds out that that we all got kicked out of town, I don't know what that would mean for me. I've already missed my weekly phone call to him."

"Maybe you can call and not mention that part."

"I strongly doubt that would work with all the people that know what happened, including the Wilkersons. He's going to eventually find out, but I want to make sure that you are safe with your family first. Wherever you go, I want to be there too... Hey, since my mother had twin brothers, wouldn't it be funny if we had our own set of twins? How many more kids do you think we might end up having down the line?"

"*More?*" Nell declared. "Just how many more did you plan on us having? We can't even afford the *one* we are going to have in six months!"

"I was hoping to at least have eleven more," Paul joked. "Then we can have a huge family, like Henry's."

He attempted to muffle his laughter, even when Nell gave him a sharp jab with her elbow. As dark as the car was, Paul could imagine the annoyed glimpse on Nell's face, making him snicker even more.

"There is *no* way we're having *that* many kids," Nell retorted. "Do you have any idea how much pain I will have to endure to give birth? I heard it was horrible. Guess what happened to my mother when she was pregnant with my brother! She had to give birth, on her own, in her *car*! Sometimes, I have nightmares about that happening to me."

"We don't have our cars, so problem solved."

"I'm serious, Paul! I'm scared! I never gave birth before. What if I don't make it or if our baby doesn't make it?"

A dullness in his chest, Paul had a pain in the back of his throat. He breathed deeply, contemplating Nell's worries. *I don't know what to say; this is all new to me too. I wouldn't want to lose either of you. You both mean everything to me.* He nuzzled against her hair, fumbling for the right words to bring Nell comfort, and, in a way, for himself.

"Babe, you know I'd never want anything bad to happen to either of you," Paul assured her. "I'll be there every step of the way. You won't be alone; I promise. You and our baby *will* make it. Don't get frightened over something that hasn't happened. As scary as things were for your mother, she still managed to have a healthy birth with your brother, you, and your sister. Your chance of having a successful birth is just as good. That, too, is something to think about. My parents weren't even able to have any children for years before they had me. I heard that so often that I thought that I couldn't have kids. Then, when you told me that you were pregnant, it was one of the happiest days of my life. I know a lot of people our age think that would be terrible news, but not me. I'm grateful to be having a baby on the way with you and I want the both of you to come out on top of this."

Holding her close, Paul gave her a supportive kiss, eager to lighten the mood within the car. Nell leaned against Paul's shoulder as they continued to watch the baseball game.

Chapter 7

For the next three days, Paul and Henry worked at the auto shop while Nell worked at the restaurant. Mr. Holiday paid Paul and Henry with most of their income being paid under the table, which did not amount to much since their lodging took up most of the money. Nevertheless, Paul and Nell took what little funds they earned to make phone calls in phone booths to speak to telephone operators to help locate Nell's family in Illinois and Michigan after their shifts at work. Even so, all they had were names and states, not phone numbers nor addresses. This meant that Paul and Nell had difficulties getting directory assistance from the telephone operators who needed an address to look up the information to connect them.

Frustrated, Paul had the inclination to slam the phone down numerous times, striving to keep his nerves under control. He began jotting down the addresses of the wrong people so that he could at least do a process of elimination and get closer to the correct address when dealing with a new operator. Some of the phones continued to ring and others expressed that he had the wrong number, not having any relation to Nell's family. Furthermore, Paul would write down the addresses to the missed calls, hoping that by chance, he would get a second response at his phone call at a different time during the day after work.

"You're wasting your time and money trying to locate her family," Henry told Paul, after work. He took a long swig of his cigarette. He closed his eyes and exhaled the smoke.

"You have a lot of nerve talking to me about money," Paul fired back, hanging up the phone after another failed attempt. "You could quit today and drive on into Florida, yet you are still here, wasting money on smokes."

"My money, I can do whatever I want with it," Henry countered. "I'm not in any rush to get back with them. Last time I talked to my folks, they kept on demanding that I hurry up and get to Florida. All they want is a free babysitter. Every time I babysit those rascals, my folks always end up having another one. I told them I have to keep working here to repair my car. Plus, the smokes aren't expensive. You can get them out of any vending machine."

"Your car has been fixed days ago," Paul said snickering. "What happened to, 'We can just leave and go to my great aunt's place in Florida and start all over.'"

"I never said anything about starting over and babysitting other people's kids."

"Those are your siblings!"

"You got that right. *Siblings*, not *my* kids. If you want to watch *ten* kids all by yourself, go for it."

Both teens laughed, getting back into Henry's car. Paul wondered what became of his well-kept red and white vehicle that had been given to him on his sixteenth birthday as a gift from his grandfather. He had worked so hard to make sure that it was taken care of and now, it was all but a ghost in his memory. He reminisced how thrilled he was when he first got it. Brand new, the car was breathtaking and was something Paul and his friends had only seen in their car magazines. He had used it often on his many dates and drives. He missed it, wishing that he had the chance to take it with him before he left.

Driving around with Henry wasn't too bad. They both still managed to find isolated roads in Magnolia where they would take some time to speed down the streets, going as fast as the car would take them. It was entertaining and made their blood pump fast throughout their veins. The best part was when Henry would do his ruthless swerves and turns. Paul roared boisterously as Henry pressed his foot heavily against the accelerator, reminding him of the one time they accidentally got caught speeding by a police officer. Not wanting to pay a hefty fine, Henry zoomed down the street in a hot pursuit with the officer, taking as many sharp turns down the street as possible. Ultimately, Henry managed to outdrive the officer. Yet, he still got a ticket because everyone in

Wood Oak knew what car he drove and knew his reputation for speeding.

"Don't expect me to pay another one of your tickets," Mr. Wilkerson bellowed at Henry, once, in front of his friends. *"You pay the ticket yourself or don't expect to drive for the rest of the school year!"*

When not practicing or attending the school games, Henry had to rake out the lawnmower, cut grass, or do other things to earn money to pay his fines. Another way the Wilkerson teen would earn his keep was working with his father as a "shade tree mechanic" to repair other people's automobiles for simple things like pumpkin pie, smokes, or other items instead of money, if the person was unable to pay. The Wilkersons would do that at other people's homes or at their own. Paul, himself, did it on rare occasions as well.

After a long, wild drive, Henry and Paul returned to Mr. Holiday's house. Only this time, the home smelled remarkably delicious, like there was actual food! Henry and Paul rushed to the kitchen, finding Mr. Holiday digging a fork into a plate of freshly made lasagna. Paul could smell the savory onions, garlic, meat, and cheese, making his mouth water.

"That smells good," Henry stated. "Where'd you get that from?"

"Tracy and Nell brought it over fifteen minutes ago," Mr. Holiday said. "There's a whole pan of it next to the stove!"

Real food and not a sandwich sounded like music to Paul's ears. *Thank you, Nell, for thinking about us and caring that we get a wholesome meal tonight.*

Chapter 8

On Saturday, in the phone booth, Paul stood by, listening while the phone rang. It was five o'clock in the evening and he was anxious. The garage had been busy all day with him unloading the tire truck, restocking inventory, and washing windshields. Next Monday, Mr. Holiday was going to have him and Henry assist the mechanics by checking oil and checking the tire air pressures, as needed. They were slowly progressing into having more complex duties. Paul was just about to hang up the phone until there was a *click* at the other end of the line.

"Hello?" a deep masculine voice on the other end of the line answered.

"Hello," Paul said, straightening his slumped posture. "I'm trying to locate Harold and Shirley Jefferson."

"Who wants to know?" the man asked.

"My name is Paul Boudreaux and I'm trying to locate my girlfriend's parents. They used to live in Wood Oak, Louisiana and my girlfriend's name is Nell Jefferson."

"Nell's my niece from down in Louisiana," the man said. "My brother, his wife, and kids came up here a few days ago without her. They filed a missing person's report, but we haven't heard anything...She's your *girlfriend*, you say? Hold on, I'm going to ask my wife to go a few doors down the hallway to get my brother. He should be home right about now."

There was a prolonged pause.

"Hello," a different masculine voice answered, after what must have been several minutes.

"Hi, Mr. Jefferson. My name is Paul Boudreaux. I'm Nell's boyfriend. Nell is safe and she is with me in Louisiana. I've been trying to locate you all for a while--."

"*Boyfriend?*" Mr. Jefferson bellowed, bitterness in his voice. "So, *you're* the white boy my daughter has been sneaking around with! Nell needs to come here and be with her family. She isn't safe down there in Louisiana and neither are you."

"I know, but we got stranded in Magnolia. We found some nice people to help us out. Now that I know how to contact you, she and I can work on going up there to Illinois. It might take us a few more days."

"Is that so? What do you plan on doing once she is here with us? She can't keep seeing you."

"Sir, I would like to keep seeing her. She means the world to me and with your blessing, I would like to marry her."

"*Marry her?* No, you two need to go your separate ways. Nothing good would ever come of your relationship. You being white, you'll be accepted anywhere as long as nobody finds out that you were with a Negro girl. Nell needs to be with us and finish school."

"Mr. Jefferson, I don't want to keep being separated from Nell. I love her and don't see myself ever letting her go, regardless of how anyone else feels about us. She and I are expecting to have a baby together in a few months; wouldn't it be appropriate for us to remain together seeing that I am the father and choosing to stay because I want to be with them?"

"A *baby*! Lord have mercy… Aren't you part of the Boudreaux family that everyone talks badly about in Wood Oak? Nell had no business getting caught up with boys; I told her that many times so she wouldn't be in the situation she is in now. Expecting a baby…She ruined her life… She knows better, especially knowing where we lived."

"Yes, sir, but I don't have anything to do with my family. If that were the case, I'd still be in Wood Oak. I take responsibility and will do everything possible to fully support Nell and the baby."

"Where is Nell presently?"

"She is at a friend's house. I am going there in a few minutes. I can let her know that I talked to you and make arrangements for her to speak to you herself tomorrow. Would this same time be the best time to call you tomorrow?"

"Yes, I'll make sure the rest of the family is here when she calls. Let me give you our direct phone number for her to call…"

After jotting the information down with a paper and pen and hanging up the phone, Paul walked back to Henry's smoke infused automobile. Henry had his eyes closed with a cigarette held between two fingers. He, too, was still in his coveralls listening to the rock and roll music that blasted from the car radio. When the next song began, he opened his eyes and turned the radio dial to the different channels, not liking any of the music that played.

"We really should invest in getting a record player and getting some new 45s and 78s," Henry said. "Luke told me that the record store on Howell Boulevard has the best selections. He and I are going to the bowling alley this evening to hang out with a few of his friends, you want to join us?"

"Nah, I'm spending time with Nell," replied Paul. "Speaking of that, can I borrow your car tonight and Monday after work?"

"You better be careful with taking my car down to the colored area, as often as you go. You're going to start drawing attention to yourself again and get us both in trouble. I'm gonna head back to the house, shower, and change clothes. You can drop me off at the bowling alley. I can catch a ride back home with Luke."

After the friends went back to Mr. Holiday's home, they showered and changed clothes. Paul dropped Henry off at the bowling alley and drove down to Mrs. Ann's house. Unfortunately, Nell was not there. She and Tracy went to the Baptist church for bible study and wouldn't be back for another hour.

Oh wait, Paul thought. She did tell me that she would be going. I forgot that it was tonight. I'll just head back to the bowling alley and join Henry and the rest of the guys.

Paul returned to the bowling alley just in time to find Henry, Luke, and few unknown faces gathered in the middle lane of the building. Seeing him, Henry waved him over. Paul paid his fees and got some bowling shoes. He spotted a green bowling ball and took it off the rack, heading down to the area where Henry and the others were.

"Guess common sense decided to kick in," Henry laughed. "Paul, meet Brian Anderson and Trenton Grimes. You already know Luke."

Brian was a nineteen-year-old, tall, well-built teen with medium, shoulder length blonde hair and brown eyes. He wore solid white pants, a green and yellow shirt, and brown shoes. Trenton was a thin, eighteen-year-old, with feathered strawberry blonde hair and green eyes. He wore solid brown paints with a solid red shirt and black shoes.

"Is this everyone?" Paul asked Henry who was putting the names onto the scoreboards.

"Nah, we got one more player," Henry corrected him. "Dylan Matthews is heading this way."

An eighteen-year-old with short curly brown hair and blue eyes joined them. He had blue jeans, a solid yellow shirt, and brown shoes.

"You, me, and Luke are going to win this bet," Henry informed Paul, keying in the last name and putting on his bowling shoes.

"What bet?"

"Whichever team has the person with the highest score gets the money," Henry said. "You got five bucks to add?"

"Are you nuts?" Paul whispered. "We hardly have any money as is!"

"Or we could double it," Henry responded. "You wanna get some extra change to take your old lady out, right? Well, you can do it with the extra money if we win.

It's like someone else is paying for your date. It's not like you're betting a fortune."

"How do we know if we can even beat these guys? You think *thoughts* of winning money can miraculously make us better?"

"It sure can," Henry said. "Luke's gone bowling with these guys before and he said that they aren't any good, so we are guaranteed to win! Easy money! Are you in or out?"

Paul contemplated Henry's offer. He wasn't that great at bowling himself, but he wanted something fun to do after working so diligently that day. Tilting his head from side to side, weighing his options, Paul spoke.

"Ok, I'm in," Paul told his friend. "For one game. Then, I must leave. This better not be a setup where we put out money and these guys end up being ringers. Why would they bet on a game, knowing they can't bowl?"

"Great," Henry spoke, watching Paul put on his bowling shoes. "They don't know us, and we don't know them. It's a gamble either way. Give Dylan the money. He is holding everyone's wagers."

Paul took out his wallet, opened it, and gave five dollars to Dylan. Stuffing his wallet back into his pants pocket, he watched Henry grab his red bowling ball and rolled it down the lane. Everyone held their breaths as the ball moved, ending in a strike!

"Yeah," Henry hollered, drawing the attention of most of the people in the bowling alley. He walked back to his team with a fast-paced strut before giving Paul a high five.

Brian grasped his blue bowling ball. He rolled it down the ally, knocking down eight bowling pins. He grimaced, while Henry gave a mocking cheer. Brian grumbled and grabbed his bowling ball again. He rolled it down the alley once more, hitting only one pin.

"Ha!" Henry teased as Luke began his turn.

"This is going to be interesting," Paul murmured, watching Luke also make a strike.

Next, it was Trenton's turn. He rolled his orange bowling ball down the lane, knocking down only five pins. Paul and the rest of his team chuckled as Trenton sought in vain to hit more pins once his ball returned, only for it to instantly go into the gutter.

With his turn, Paul took his green bowling ball and rolled it down the lane. The bowling ball moved, knocking down eight pins. Regrettably, he did not take down more pins on his second attempt.

Dylan gripped his blue bowling ball and was just about to take his turn until there was a thunderous sound coming from a neighboring lane.

BAM!

A purple bowling ball had slammed onto the floor and out of the hand of a blonde hair, blue eyed teen girl who must have been no older than sixteen. She had on a solid light blue blouse, white pants, and multicolored bowling shoes. The other teenage girls in the same group as the blonde covered their mouths with their hands in shock as the girl's bowling ball, diagonally, crossed over into Paul's groups lane, then the neighboring lane, and another lane. The ball crashed into the pinsetter just as it was about to clear a set of fallen pins on the pin deck.

Instantly, Paul, his friends, and several other onlookers burst into laughter. Dylan clutched his bowling ball tightly towards his stomach as he leaned forward to chuckle. Paul laughed so hard that he smacked Henry on the back, who in turn almost fell out of his chair from snickering. Luke grabbed ahold of his sides as tears began to run down his cheeks.

"Oh my gosh, Molly," one of the girl's friends cried. "I'm so embarrassed for you!"

The purple bowling ball went back towards the middle of the affected bowling lane, pausing its dramatic roll. One of the bowling alley's staff retrieved the ball, handing it back to the blonde who was now flushed in the cheeks from mortification.

"H-hey," Henry gasped to Dylan in the middle of his snicker. He sunk down towards the ground, trying to regain his stance. His chest quivered the longer he laughed. "Hurry up and bowl before those mirror warmers mess up your game."

"Give me a minute," Dylan said still guffawing.

Regaining his composure, Henry grabbed his red bowling ball and hurled it down the lane, knocking down seven pins. While he was waiting for his ball to return, he noticed that the girl named Molly was about to redo her turn. He swore under his breath, praying for his ball to return before the girl went again. Regrettably, his ball didn't return in time. The girl flung her ball down the lane; it directly went into the gutter.

With his ball back in play, Henry seized his red bowling ball.

"Hey," he called over to Molly, "maybe you should just sit down and watch the experts play."

Molly's mouth dropped at Henry's crude remark. Henry rolled his ball down his lane. It rolled into the gutter.

"When a *real* expert shows up, let me know!" Molly said stomping back to rejoin her friends.

Disgraced, Henry reverted to his group's seating area. After the bowling game was completed, Henry had the highest score of 250 and Trenton having the lowest score of 90.

"Anyone want to do another game?" Henry asked getting his winnings from Dylan.

"I'm going to sit this one out," Trenton said. "I'm not that good at bowling."

"Or are you just saying that to get Henry to let his guard down," Paul joked.

"I wish," Trenton laughed. "I can't bowl to save my life. I was hoping that you would have been worse than me when you were bowling, but you got a 190."

"Bowling is not my sport," Paul admitted. "My score is usually 120 or less."

"70 is my worst score. It's normally 140; I just had a bad night."

"We all should do this again, even if it doesn't include bets. It was fun. I'm going to head out and see my old lady." Paul gathered his winnings and headed out the bowling alley.

Chapter 9

"I can't believe it," Nell said, her face upturned, Sunday afternoon. "You actually found them. Thank you so much. I am so grateful!" Her eyes sparkled and appearance relaxed.

"I'll wait here while you talk to your family," Paul said. He waited in the car while Nell entered the phone booth, using the paper Paul had given her that contained her parents' contact information. He turned on the car radio, humming to the sound of the music. He giggled to himself thinking about the funny events that occurred in the bowling alley. He couldn't believe how terrible some people were at bowling. Molly certainly beat that one girl named Vivian Donaldson who threw a fit while on a double date with Henry years ago. Vivian had broken her nail after her first attempt at bowling, choosing to lightly roll the ball into the gutter during her turn from that moment on.

Paul opened the car's glove compartment where Henry usually kept his car magazines. Most were old, but viewing the different car designs never bored him, especially the ones that had those fantastic white wall tires that made cars look extra sharp. Paul flipped through the pages, reading their descriptions, and studying their pictures with a critical eye.

When Nell came back to the car, Paul placed the magazines back into the glove compartment, and began the long drive down the road, with the windows rolled down. Paul enjoyed breathing in the fresh hair, taking it all in, living for the moment.

"How did the call go?" Paul questioned Nell, holding, and caressing her hand with his free one.

"It could have been worse," Nell replied. "My parents were upset, but they were glad to hear from me. My dad got on me about being pregnant and not finishing school, like he wanted. He said I was ruining my life and needed to go up to Illinois to get my life together. My mom told me that she would be able to help get me job. She said that they have a neighbor who has an elderly mother who could use a lot of help around her house."

"What about finishing school? Wasn't that something that was supposed to be in the works too?"

"I won't be able to finish, not while being pregnant, especially once I start to show more. I have to go to work."

"If finishing school is what you want, it can still happen. Certainly, your dreams are beyond babysitting someone else. Tell me, if you could have your dream job, what would it be?"

"I've always liked helping other people, so working with the lady would be close to that dream of being a nurse. Things aren't about me anymore. I got to think about our son or daughter and work to save what I can so he or she will have a better chance at life."

"You make it sound like you're alone. Why? I've always stated that I wanted to be there for you and our baby. Is there a reason why when you speak about your future plans that it doesn't include me?"

"I appreciate all that you do. You come and visit me all the time, risking everything again. When Bill knocked you out, I thought you were dead… What if something happens again where the next time you won't live? I don't want to put you in more danger."

"That's not true at all! Things with Bill and those jerks in Wood Oak were bound to happen because they were either greedy or ignorant. You were just a scapegoat people used to show their true colors."

Paul drove the car to a side street and parked it.

"Think about it," he persisted. "It's like football, sometimes the other team intercepts our plans and life takes us on a different path than what we expected or maybe, sometimes, we fumble on our own. All you can do is your best to take back control of what has been given to you and if you're lucky, the right people will be on your side as your defenses to help you win the game together. Sometimes you win; sometimes you lose, but life goes on and you should take every opportunity to make yourself happy. Babe, if you want to be a nurse, it can still happen. Being a young mother is no reason to throw your dreams away."

"I understand, Paul? What are your dreams?"

"To be with you."

"Are you being silly again?" Nell chortled.

"I'm here living the dream, aren't I?" Paul said grinning. "I like sports and always wanted to be a football and baseball coach. That's why when Coach Anderson found out, he had higher expectations from me than anybody else on the team. Boy, did he give me a harder time than everyone else! My grades had to be better. I had to run faster, throw the ball farther, and much more, almost to the point where I started to think he hated me. But, I knew he was doing it because he wanted me to succeed and believed in me. Even though things look bleak for now, I don't think that my dreams of being a coach are over, and neither are your dreams! Always remember that there is a way. I'll be there with you every step of the way to watch you become a nurse. So, when are your parents expecting to see us in Illinois?"

"They wanted me to be there as soon as possible. I told them it all depended on you and Henry because I have no other means of getting there, unless I took the bus or train."

"Henry and I talked about hitchhiking a few days ago," Paul joked before Nell rolled her eyes laughing. She looked down at the car radio, smiling at the happy tune that was playing.

"I like this song," Nell said, singing along to the chorus, and waving a finger in the air like a conductor's wand. Paul joined her, both laughing.

Chapter 10

The following Saturday afternoon, Paul was hanging out with his guy friends at the basement of Trenton's parents' home watching the latest professional baseball game.

Paul had already told everyone that he would be moving to Illinois, with Henry taking a few days off from the job to bring him up north. Wanting to spend more time together, the guys decided to hang out for fun one last time together at Trenton's house. There, the basement seemed like a standard mancave with a television, couch, rug, posters, and various random things such as trunks, old lamps, and other knickknacks. On the makeshift coffee table were two big bowls of butter popcorn, cans of various sodas on top of coasters, potato chips, and finger sandwiches freshly prepared by Trenton's mother. The guys' attention was centered on the game and the teams who were at play, mainly because they were in the middle of yet another wager on which team would prevail. So far, the team that Paul, Luke, and Brian were betting on was losing, making them more on edge as time ticked on.

Knock! Knock!

Squinting his eyes and swatting at the air at the bothersome noise coming from the entrance of the basement door, Trenton sprinted up the stairs, opening the door to see his sixteen-year-old sister glaring at him.

"I have a test on Monday that I have to study for," she whined. "It's your turn to watch Katy and Avery tonight!"

"I'm watching the game with the guys," Trenton argued. "You still owe me for the time I watched them when you wanted to go shopping with your friends!"

"I *had* to! Valerie has a hot brother that was coming to town the next day!"

"Then get *them* to help you," Trenton grumbled.

"As if," his sister barked, "I have to pass this test or else my teacher is going to call mom and dad about my grades slipping again. Can't you just help me one more time? Please!"

Trenton's hand temporarily clenched before he pressed his fist to his mouth. Hesitantly, he expanded the door, permitting his six- year-old sister and four-year-old brother into the basement.

"You two better *not* make a sound," Trenton whispered, displeasure in his tone. Both kids dashed down the stairs heading to the bowls of popcorn. Incensed at the presence of the youngsters, Henry and Brian shot Trenton pinched expressions with their faces upon his arrival back to the couch.

Reaching in the bowl to get more popcorn, four-year-old, Avery inadvertently tipped the bowl over, spilling the popcorn over the table and the floor.

"Oh, come on, kid," Brian objected kicking the fallen popcorn away from his feet.

Avery and Katy began picking up the popcorn. Avery grabbed a few more pieces but started putting them into his mouth.

"Don't eat off the floor," Paul told him, making a sour face, and pushing the child's hand away from his face to prevent him from stuffing his face more. Paul began grabbing a few pieces of fallen popcorn nearby, placing them back into the bowl. Unexpectedly, Katy tilted her head back and jerked it forward, letting out a noisy sneeze, along with a long, slimy, string of green snot that landed from her nose onto the back of Paul's popcorn filled hand. Cringing, Paul released the popcorn back into the bowl.

"Ugh," he hollered, snatching a paper towel to wipe his hand.

"Where are your parents?" Henry screeched to Trenton, visible tension in his neck, shoulders, and arms.

"They are on one of their dates," Trenton replied, grabbing a paper towel and cleaning his sister's nose. He turned to Paul, "Sorry about that."

"Let's finish watching the game at Holiday's," Henry proposed to everyone. "There's a smaller television screen, but nobody will bother us there."

"We can't," Trenton refuted. "I'm watching the kids, remember."

"Yeah, you, not us."

"Hey, quiet down you two, O'Reilly is about to bat," Paul said to them, his eyes glued to the screen.

All the bases were loaded, and the batter came up to bat. The pitcher threw the ball. O'Reilly swung the bat, hitting the ball, making a homerun.

Paul, Luke, and Brian sprang from their places on the couch, cheering. Their team won! Katy and Avery joined in the merriment, unaware of their brother's situation. Henry and Trenton were flabbergasted. Henry began to swear under his breath. Trenton kicked at the ground with his feet.

"Trenton," Henry said, a sudden stillness in his face but visible tension in his jawline, "your sister better pass that test."

Chapter 11

Before returning home that evening, Paul had Henry drive him to a phone booth. Reluctantly, Paul entered the booth, his legs and knees weak. He pushed the coins through the slot and dialed the number he had been dreading for the past few days. There was a sinking feeling in his stomach, the longer he stood there. He was a week behind on his required call, but it was a first for him, praying that it would not be that big of a deal. Regardless, he had everything planned. Tomorrow he planned on being long gone by the time anyone would be able to prevent him from going to Illinois with Henry and Nell. Mr. Holiday had already been notified that Henry would be dropping them off for the next few days. Paul hated that he would be leaving his new friends and associates, but he owed it to Nell to get her home safely and be there for her and their baby. That was his number one priority, with the hope that one day, they could come back and visit Magnolia when the time was right. Rubbing the back of his neck, Paul listened to the rings until there was a click at the other end of the phone.

"Hello," answered the recognizable voice at the other end.

"Uncle Simon… it's Paul…"

"You are late with your call and haven't been showing up to school as agreed."

"I know and I'm sorry. There were some complications in Wood Oak, and I didn't know if I could call you or not, after what happend there."

"I know *everything* that went on in Wood Oak," Simon said. "Unlike you, the Wilkerson family informed me that you all were expelled from the parish and had to leave with their son. That's why I wanted you to go to the Whittington School for Boys in Alabama months ago. The Wilkerson family and you have proven to be incapable of managing your affairs. I will be taking charge from this moment forward. You, Paul, will be coming to Alabama where you belong."

"I can't go with you! I have a girlfriend who needs me!"

"Your concerns regarding girls are of no importance to me."

There was a click at the other end of the phone, indicating that Simon had ended the phone call. Paul dropped his head with his eyes closed on the verge of tears. Tightening his hands into a fist, Paul struck the metallic part of the phone booth. Pain surged through his hand, but he didn't care. Paul stormed out the phone booth, crossing the street back into Henry's vehicle.

"What's bothering you?" Henry asked, shoving an unlit cigarette into his mouth. He passed the cigarette pack to Paul, who shook his head. Using his lighter, Henry lit his cigarette, put the lighter and pack away, and restarted the drive

"My uncle," Paul told him, letting out a strangled cry of frustration. "He knows about what happened in Wood Oak. I think we need to leave tonight."

"Tonight," Henry objected, "Have you forgotten how late it is? Aren't you tired? We all agreed to leave tomorrow!"

Paul's posture stooped. He folded his arms across his stomach. He was drained, physically, and mentally, so much so that his eye lids were heavy. He thought about Henry's words weighing in if he and Nell should leave on their own with bus tickets, but, what if Nell didn't want to leave that evening either when they already made plans to leave the following morning?

"You're right," Paul agreed, closing his eyes. "I'll get us breakfast after we pick up Nell. It'll have to be from one of the fast-food joints because we got to leave fast. I don't know what I'm going to do about finding a place in Illinois. Maybe I can find another person who rents out rooms."

"Don't you turn eighteen in two weeks?"

"Yeah, but my uncle doesn't care about any of that. I hope that the Jeffersons will at least consider letting me marry Nell. If I can hide out long enough, I won't even need Simon's permission to marry once I turn eighteen.

Also, he will have no choice but to give me some of my trust fund. That should help me and Nell out until we find a better place to stay together." Paul took out the paper that contained the address and telephone number to the Jeffersons and placed it into the glove compartment.

"What you got there?" Henry asked.

"The address and number to Nell's family," Paul said. "I'm putting it there, so it won't get lost. Last thing we need is to lose that information. I hate that we must leave Magnolia! I like this place, you know that."

"Me too," Henry agreed. "I'm going to drop you two off and head back. I might go to night school or just join the military."

"We both have to sign up for selective service regardless," Paul laughed. "Hey, since we both are going to be eighteen soon, we should use the buddy system when we join the marine corp. If they should pull either of our names, at least we get to be together too."

"When you turn eighteen, be on the right side of the map. Everything on the west of the Mississippi goes to California and everything on the east goes to South Carolina."

"We got to be at the same place too when we sign up. Let's talk about it more tomorrow; I'm beat."

"Sure, pal."

Chapter 12

Next morning, everything was packed in the suitcases that Mr. Holiday had given them. In his suitcase, Paul packed a few articles of clothing and necessities such as toiletries and his toothbrush. Henry had finished packing and was waiting for Paul near the entrance to the home. The moment was bittersweet. Paul was going to miss spending time with the guys who had made his time in Magnolia a pleasant one, missing the bowling alley and gatherings in the basement of their homes. Locking onto the memories, Paul promised himself that he would never forget them.

"Here's a little something for your trip," Mr. Holiday said, handing the teen a small roll of dollar bills.

"Sir, you don't have to," Paul began.

"But I do," Mr. Holiday said. "You did a great job working for me and are welcomed back anytime. Don't stay gone too long."

"Thank you," Paul said giving the elder a brief hug, missing the man already.

Paul made his way out of the home, walking with Henry to the vehicle's open trunk. Henry placed his belongings inside, leaving room for Paul to do the same. Beaming, Paul lifted his suitcase, placing it inside, and closing the trunk. Visible gooseflesh on his arms and almost shivering with pleasure, Paul couldn't wait to see the new adventure the drive would take him and his loved ones.

"Let's pick up Nell and get going," Henry spoke climbing into the driver's seat. Next to him, Paul slid into the front passenger side. He began rolling down the window, desiring for the wind to playfully dance between strands of his black hair. Henry started the car, backing out of the driveway.

Suddenly, a black car pulled forward, blocking their exit. Henry slammed onto the breaks, stopping his car from smashing into the other. Three men dressed in black business suits and dark shades climbed out of the black vehicle, surrounding Henry's car. One of the men tapped on the glass window of the driver's side, making Henry roll down his window slightly.

"Paul will be going away with us," the man stated.

Almost forgetting to breathe, Paul's body tensed. His skin becoming sweaty. The second man pressed his hand in the place where the window had been rolled down. He pushed back his jacket pulling out a hidden gun that had been placed in a holster.

"Oh, yeah, where to?" Henry demanded.

"His uncle in Alabama," the first man replied. "It is time for him to leave."

"Over my dead body," Henry bellowed, grabbing the stick shift to change it, but the third man already had his pistol revealed pointing it towards Henry's head. Shocked, Henry shouted out an obscenity, backing away from the window.

"I'll just go," Paul told them, regaining his composure. "Just don't harm him!"

"Paul, you can't go with them," Henry contended.

"I don't want to, but if it means saving your life, then I will," Paul said, climbing out of the vehicle with his hands slightly raised.

Henry tried to exit as well, but the first man shut the door, shaking his head, preventing the teen from withdrawing.

"You will be staying here," he instructed Henry.

"What about my things?" Paul asked the men.

"You won't need them," the first man said.

A pain in his chest and feelings of hopelessness almost paralyzing him, Paul chocked back a sob that escaped his lips. He wiped away the tears that began were beginning to uncontrollably fall from his eyes.

"Henry," Paul spoke, his voice almost breaking. "I won't be able to tell Nell goodbye but promise me...to get her to her family safely in Illinois and tell her, I love her, and will find a way to be with her again."

Powerless, Henry could only watch Paul reluctantly follow two of the men back into the black car. The first man stayed behind, removing a hidden sharp knife from his jacket. He stabbed the front left tire of Henry's car. The tire flattened quickly as the man pulled the knife back into his pocket. Tossing what appeared to be money on the ground, he moved back to the black car, getting inside. The car took off with Paul within.

Chapter 13

The lengthy drive to Alabama was a silent one. Paul was tempted to pound the men to a pulp, but he was sandwiched between two of the armed men in the back seat. He frowned, thinking about Nell and not being able to say farewell to her. He stared out the front window, gazing at the long road ahead.

Hours later, Paul drew his limbs closer to his body. The car drove off the interstate and deep into a long, almost twisty highway leading into a heavily wooded area. The car stopped at a brilliant metallic gate that was guarded. The gate opened revealing a private lake, sculptured bushes, extravagantly landscaped flower beds, and oak trees. Almost two miles deeper into the property stood an elaborate mansion. Moving forward, the car stopped at the entrance. Near the door stood a middle-aged man, dressed in a black tuxedo, black shoes, and white gloves.

Paul left the vehicle with his captors. They walked to the entrance where the man opened the door, allowing them inside. Within the mansion was a luxurious golden grand staircase that led to a second floor. At the base of the stairs were two adjacent marbled statues of what appeared to be beautiful women. Nearby were corridors of more rooms that had closed doors. The staircase steps were marbled with a red carpet in the middle, leading up the stairs where a large portrait of an elderly man was placed. Standing at the base of the stairs were two rows of maids and butlers standing across from one another with their heads bowed submissively. At the top of the stairs in front of the portrait stood Paul's captor, his uncle, Simon Dupont. His dull hazel eyes met Paul's. Simon wore a tailor-made black suit with a red necktie and white handkerchief tucked in his upper left suit pocket. His greying strawberry blonde hair was neatly brushed back in a professional contour style and his pencil mustache was neatly trimmed.

Paul stared at his uncle's unsmiling face, knowing the life and people he treasured were now gone.

Chapter 14

Nell

With her suitcase near her feet, Nell sat in a small wooden chair on the front porch, fidgeting. Each time another vehicle would drive by, her heart would race, searching to see if the right car was heading her way. Paul had told her that they would be coming to pick her up that morning at around 7 a.m., but it was nearing 9 a.m., unlike his usual promptness.

Biting down on her lip, her mind began to think of Paul's arrival, making her heart skip a beat. She could see him approaching her with that same mischievous twinkle in his grey eyes and flirtatious smug smile. Getting flushed, Nell tried to think of something else, but the thoughts persisted. She began to imagine Paul pressing his lips together to whistle to the sound of a song being played on the radio. The closer his steps were, the wider his grin would get before giving her more of his passionate kisses. As much as Nell never wanted to admit, Paul's kisses blew her away. It was part of a spirited, coquettish game to him, to see how much he could make her melt, winning every time. At times, Nell would pretend that she wasn't interested in his enticing nature with her, but even that was something Paul enjoyed being a participant in, coming up with ways to continuously make her fall more in love with him.

In Nell's lap was a small tin container of chocolate chip cookies that Mrs. Ann had made for the long trip ahead. Opening the container, Nell bit into one of the cookies, enjoying its chocolaty taste. The cookie was soft, almost melting in her mouth. Still, time went on.

Thirty minutes later, Nell closed the tin container and began her stroll to the backyard fence. She passed the tree where Paul had kissed her days before, bringing a small, soothing smile to her face. Squeezing between the boards of the fence, Nell entered the back lot of the restaurant. She made her way to the front, opening the door to the entrance, and viewing the restaurant's regular diners who exchanged acknowledgements. Nell noticed Tracy at one of the tables, taking an order.

"Sorry to bother you," Nell whispered to her. "But would you happen to have Mr. Holiday's number?"

"I don't know his private phone number off the top of my head, but you could look in the phone book or ask a telephone operator," Tracy said, tucking her pen behind her ear. "I'd get the number to his shop because he should be there and not home at this time. It's Holiday's Garage on Flor De Lis Street."

Nodding, Nell left the restaurant, walking across the street to a phone booth that was being used. She waited until the person left, placing a few coins into the slot. She requested for the operator to connect her to Holiday's Garage, but nobody answered.

Worried, Nell rushed back to the backyard of Mrs. Ann's house. There, she heard a car horn blaring. Sprinting to the front of the home, Nell saw Henry's car parked outside along the street. Her fears lessening, Nell hurried to the vehicle expecting Paul to come out. Instead, the car only had a cantankerous, sour faced Henry inside. He blasted his horn at her, making Nell jump back slightly from the startling noise.

Where is Paul, Nell pondered, her eyes growing pained. She began to back away.

Barring his teeth and glaring at her with unsympathetic eyes, Henry flung open the door to the driver's seat. His face was red and frightening.

"What are you waiting for?" Henry bellowed. "Get in the car!"

Her body quaking, Nell backed away from him the closer he got. Increasingly irritable, Henry made his way up the stairs where Nell's luggage was. Grabbing them, he stomped down the stairs, slamming them down near the back of their ride. He opened the trunk, hurling the luggage inside before slamming the trunk lid down.

"W-where's Paul?" Nell asked, cringing at Henry's temperament.

"As if *you'd* care," Henry answered, sarcastic in voice. "You coming or what? I have better things to do than chauffer you around town." Climbing back into the car, he slammed the door shut.

Unenthusiastically, Nell approached the car, opening the right passenger door and climbing inside. She barely closed the door when the car started to burn rubber down the street.

"Is Paul coming?" Nell inquired.

"Does it *look* like he's coming with us?" Henry muttered, an edge to his tone. "And you're paying for this trip: gas, food, every damn thing! It's enough I had to get a new tire to pick you up. Don't think for a minute that I'm going to start kissing your ass. Paul was taken away to go to Alabama. Once I finish dropping you off, I'm heading that way to find him."

"Alabama? Why?"

"His uppity rich uncle, that's who."

"Then take me there. I'm not going to Illinois without Paul."

"You're going to Illinois," Henry argued. "You already ruined Paul's life, and I know what type of person you are: money hungry. Paul doesn't want to see it, but I can! I bet all that talk about him getting you knocked up isn't even true. How many guys have you been with besides him? Plenty I bet!"

"He's the only person I've ever been with…"

"Yeah right! What girl would still a virgin in the 12th grade?"

"I was…"

Henry rolled his eyes, rapping his fingers against the stirring wheel.

"And I'm not money hungry," Nell continued, her voice angry. "Anything I've ever gotten, I worked hard to get it. I never asked Paul nor anyone else to ever give me anything. I never intended for anything horrible to happen to him or anyone else."

"That's why you should have just gone to a different school! Everything was fine until you came along!"

"I tried, but the other schools were full, and my parents barely had time to help me, and my siblings register. My mother cleans houses all day and my father was busy doing odd jobs around town since the company he worked for closed. They were busier with trying to get a means of putting food on the table and making sure we had what we need to survive. All the other schools in other parishes were already integrated, so why not Wood Oak High School."

Henry stopped the car in front of the red-light signal. He looked at her through his rearview mirror noticing the school ring that hung on Nell's golden necklace. He snorted.

"Nancy was hoping to get that ring," Henry said, a sharp tone in his voice. "How'd you manage to get it? The guys and I never thought Paul would give his ring to anybody, and she was with him for years. What's so special about you?"

"He said he loved me more than her."

"What about that guy named Martin? Didn't you have a thing for him?"

"No, he was more like a friend to me. I'm sure you don't love every single white girl that's out there yourself."

"You got that right. The only girl I ever really liked was this mirror warmer named Deirdre Chapman. I was crazy about her, that is until she left me for another guy on the team who ended up using her as much as she used me. I took her back, twice, until I got tired of it all."

"What ended up happening to them?"

"The guy moved away before school started this year. Deirdre still attends Wood Oak, but we don't talk."

The light turned green, and the car began to move again.

"How did you and Paul meet?" Nell asked.

"When his father was alive, he used to hire people around town who needed work at Sal's, including my dad. Everyone liked working there and Mr. Boudreaux would always make sure that everyone was taken care of and paid on time. He was laid back, long as you did your job and helped each other out with no drama attached. If anyone did anything to make him mad, he usually gave only one more chance, then the person was out, but it would be their fault, not his. If he had no more work, he'd network with other businesses to get people jobs or would have them sell things at Sal's. He would always find a way to help. Paul and I met at the store, found out he liked the same things I did, met up a few times at the park, and been hanging out ever since. When his father passed away, his grandfather took over everything and got rid of all the workers who weren't Boudreauxs. He closed parts of the store too. That made everyone mad, but they still went to Sal's because of Paul's father and what he had done while he was alive. People began to struggle and Paul's grandfather, who had a loan business saw to it that people were in debt to him, charging them all these crazy fees. Sometimes, he would make deals and have people go after others to take off some of the burden, but it only made things worse. He was recording everything in this dumb book he calls 'The Album' and had been doing it for years. He controlled everyone and we were all miserable. The only time anyone had any relief was when Paul began assisting his grandfather. He convinced the old man to let a few people start selling a few things in the store in exchange for a low percentage or lowered the fees, but it still wasn't the same as when his father was in charge."

"But they were the same people who betrayed him."

"That's because his Uncle Harry scared everyone into thinking that Paul would turn against them by using The Album to be with you. Everyone knows that his grandfather had the book and Paul had been living with him for years. Now, the one person who cared more about the community can't go back to the parish that he grew up in."

Nell pressed her lips together before letting out a deep sigh.

"We can go to Alabama and search for him. Why not work together?"

"No," Henry said. "This is one promise to him that I intend to keep: taking you to your folks. It's the least I can do for him."

Chapter 15

The remainder of the trip towards Illinois wasn't as conversational. Henry turned on the radio to listen to rock and roll music, between his smokes. Crossing the different state lines, they would pass the welcome signs surrounded by different travelers who would be taking pictures with their friends or family. Along the way there were hitchhikers and vacationers. Most of the scenery was photogenic with trees, lakes, and architectural buildings.

The only time Henry would stop was to refuel the automobile, use the restroom, eat, or to rest up. Nell offered to drive, but Henry refused, parking the car near a shady area. When the sun began to set, Henry parked the car in the parking lot of a restaurant connected to a truck stop. He slept in the front while Nell slept in the backseat.

The next day, the driving resumed with the drive ending in Saralyn, Illinois many hours later. The buildings were taller and busier with the crowds of people coming and going. The streets were filled with cars, crowding available spaces, and moving at a crawling pace. Car horns blasted between irritated drivers and the sidewalks were filled with people busily coming and going.

"Alabama is a whole state," Nell said to Henry. "What if you can't find Paul by yourself?"

"Then I will wait until he contacts me," Henry responded. "They can't hold him hostage forever." He inched the car further, blowing his horn. "Good luck living here with all this traffic." Rolling down his car window, he flagged down a nearby bystander who was drinking from a soda can. "Hey, where is Brooks Street?"

"How the hell should I know," the bystander replied.

"You *live* here, you idiot," Henry responded.

Taking one last slip, the bystander removed his lips from the can, hurling it at Henry's car. The can hit the side of Henry's car, bounced to the side of a nearby trashcan, and fell on the ground.

Cracking his knuckles, Henry turned the car engine off, threw the driver's door open, getting out of the vehicle. Startled, the bystander began to take off by foot. Picking up the fallen can, Henry hurled it towards the man, missing him, and hitting the side of a business, barely avoiding hitting another onlooker.

The cars behind Henry's began blaring their horns.

"Shut up," Henry shouted, getting back into the vehicle, restarting the engine, and driving up a few inches more.

"Maybe he actually didn't know where the street was," Nell stated.

"Then, that's what he gets for not knowing anything," Henry replied.

Paying close attention to the street signs, they drove more until Nell noticed that one read, Brooks Street. She alerted Henry who turned the automobile into the street, driving sluggishly.

The drive ended in front of a tall ten-story, brick, apartment building in a crowded, lower middle-class neighborhood, the exact address written down. Parked cars took up majority of the street, leaving no room for other vehicles to park along the narrow street. Stopping the car in front of the building, Henry exhaled as Nell climbed out, gathering her belongings. On the stoop of the building sat a small group of Negro men in their early twenties wearing trendy, bright colored clothing and shoes. Most had medium length afros that stood high and wide. They were deep into their conversation, ignoring all of the other people who walked past.

Putting her bags on the sidewalk and approaching the front passenger door, Nell opened it with a small opening.

"When you find Paul, you'll tell me, right?" she asked.

Henry said nothing, keeping his eyes on the road. His attitude was nonchalant, shrugging half-heartedly. Frowning, Nell closed the door and gathered her belongings. She approached the building, excusing herself and squeezing past the men to enter the complex. The building was old, but in fair condition with light, faded, blue painted walls and black painted door frames. She climbed the stairs, walking to the third floor, down the hallway, and stopped at apartment 312, the address her parents had given.

Her palms sweaty, Nell knocked on the door.

Chapter 16

"Nell," exclaimed a tall, bald, middled aged Negro man, in his fifties. He was dressed in a dark green shirt, brown slacks, and black shoes. Smiling, Nell opened her arms, embracing the man. "You're back! Thank the Lord! You are still alive!"

"Dad, I called you several times and told you!" Nell grumbled.

"Nell," cried out a middle-aged Negro woman with greying hair. She wore a solid, dark solid purple dress and white shoes that were flat. "I can't believe you're back! I thought we'd never see you again!" She rushed up to Nell, hugging her with tears in her eyes.

"I am, thanks to Paul and Henry," Nell told them.

Nell entered the cozy apartment. Mr. Jefferson closed the door and sat down next to his daughter who was sitting between him and his wife. The apartment was a small two-bedroom apartment that only had bits and pieces of their old home. The pictures were old, but in new places on the wall or other surfaces. The used upholstered couch, sofa, and chair was new. There was a tiny black and white television that was new and a second-hand wooden coffee table. There were bits of neatly organized toys off to the side of the couch. Nell could tell that the couch must have been the new place where her little brother must have slept because there was a small pillow off to the side of her mother.

"So, where is Paul?" Mr. Jefferson questioned Nell, "Did he come with you to bring you home?"

"No," Nell said, a tightness in her throat and her chin trembling. "He wasn't able to come. He wanted to be here but couldn't."

"Mmm hmm," Mr. Jefferson replied, his mouth pinched with a bitter expression. "I'm not surprised. You're lucky to have made it here at all. Let this be a hard lesson learned for you. Paul wasn't honest with either of us. He said he would be here for you and the baby, yet, as we all can see, he is not. He had no genuine plans of taking responsibility for his actions. He used you and left you on your own to pick up the pieces."

Nell's demeanor quickly changed; her body quickly appearing to shrink. Her lips silently mouthing, "W-what?" She gave her father a long, pained look, before breaking eye contact.

"Paul would never do that," Nell said, her voice barely audible and shaky.

"Then explain to me why he isn't here to do all the things he promised," her father spoke.

"His family took him away..."

"Sure, they did," Mr. Jefferson said, his voice on edge. "Anything to get rid of you! Even if that were the case, deep down he must have wanted to go. Otherwise, he would be here regardless of how his family felt. It's only a matter of time until he starts to think like they do, hating Negro people. He's at that age where he is curious and wanted to see what it was like to be with a Negro girl, but you got to realize that these young white boys would never marry girls like you, especially the ones from Wood Oak. It's better that you are here away from him before he breaks your heart further."

Nell curled her toes in her shoes. She was growing nauseous, thinking about the words that were coming from her father's mouth. The tears began to flow heavily down her cheeks, the more she tried to drown out the words, but the realities of Paul's absence kept on confirming his words.

"All I ever asked of you was to make good grades and finish school," Mr. Jefferson continued. "Instead, you fooled around with boys and got pregnant. I can't believe that you allowed someone to use and rob you of a future that could have been so much better with a high school diploma. From this moment on, you are going to work, so that you will be able to help provide for your baby. After work, come straight home and under no circumstances are you allowed to go anywhere unless your mother or I know about it."

For the next four months, Nell, at seven months pregnant, worked odd jobs around Saralyn, Illinois. Like in Magnolia, she was able to find a job in a restaurant a few blocks away from home, but the manager was less sympathetic, not caring how long she or the other workers stood, sometimes causing excruciating pain in Nell's back, legs, and feet. The only time she was able to have any form of relief was when allowed to go to the bathroom. Inside the stall, Nell would grimace in agony, fighting back the urge to cry or groan. Her back hurt, extending her time within the stall.

"I-I got to leave," she uttered, rising from the seat, pain surging from her back down to her feet. Shivering and moaning, Nell grimaced, opening the stall, and washing her hands.

"The manager is looking for you," the hostess from the restaurant whispered to her when Nell left the bathroom.

Choking back a whimper, Nell moved to the back of the restaurant where the manager sat in his seat behind his desk.

"You keep staying in the bathroom for long periods of time," he said. "I need people out working, not disappearing."

"I'm sorry, but I needed to sit down," Nell said, shifting from one sore foot to the other, almost on the verge of tears.

"I'm afraid I am going to have to let you go," the manager said. "I need people who are willing to work, not wanting to sit."

With that, he motioned for her to leave. Dismayed, Nell gathered her belongings, leaving the establishment. Most jobs were like that, ending the same way. Sitting outside on a bench, she began to sob heavily. People walked by, not troubling themselves, as if she didn't exist.

Nell speculated if her parents would be disheartened in her yet again. She couldn't stay in school, couldn't get a high school diploma, couldn't keep Paul, and couldn't keep a job. She wanted to disappear and give up hope that her situation would ever change for the better. After all, everyone would just say that she did it to herself. Nell wiped away another tear with her hand, wanting to stand, but the pain continued to radiate the more she tried.

The bus she was waiting for approached the sidewalk. Forcing herself upright again, Nell stood in line to get on, each step more agonizing than the last.

"Hurry up," someone from behind whined when Nell paid her bus fare. That's the way it was, one person projecting their frustrations out on another.

Nell understood why some people slept on the bus. They too were exhausted, putting all their energy reserves into their jobs, maybe wishing to do something else, like she did. Often, Nell would think about Paul, wondering if he missed her as much as she missed him. At night, she would hold Paul's ring in her hands, remembering the time he gave it to her, and making her feel special. Nell would also think about the time they were together at the old pecan tree.

"Good looking, huh?" Paul said, motioning for Nell *to get nearer. Her heart hammering, Nell stepped closer. Tenderly, Paul's lips touched hers. "And I think you're beautiful, babe." He smirked that cocky smile that Nell had grown to love, making her wrap her arms around him.*

"You're such a romantic, Paul Boudreaux," Nell giggled.

"I can't help it, you have that effect on me," Paul whispered, giving her another kiss. "I love you, baby."

"I love you too."

Nell didn't want to doubt Paul's love for her. He had been so sweet and tender with her since they had been together. In her heart, Nell knew one thing for certain that regardless of what the future would bring, she knew with certainty that the boy who loved her during those treasured moments *did* love her and felt the same as she. Even though her father forbad her from mentioning Paul in his household, she was free to see and be with her love in her heart, thoughts, and prayers. In those scared places, she could see his happy-go-lucky smile, believing in her, as her strongest supporter.

I won't give up on him, Nell thought. *Paul wouldn't have given up on me and even if things aren't looking too great for me, I will find another way to reach my goals in life, even if it's not the path I initially chose...but Paul, I hope that path leads to you.*

Chapter 17

"You just got to keep doing the best you can," Nell's mother told her. "At one point, I had four jobs and whenever I felt tired, I just had to push those feelings aside and work harder than before."

Nell managed to get another job, days later. Her mother had spoken to a neighbor who needed someone to help care for her elderly mother while she was out working at one of the local schools. The duties were fairly light: cleaning around the house, fixing her meals, helping her to eat, and other tasks. Best of all, Nell could rest as often as needed, as long as the neighbor's mother, ninety-year-old Mrs. Betty Echols was cared for. Working for Mrs. Betty couldn't have come at a better time, raising her spirits.

Occasionally, Nell would babysit the four-year-old Williams brothers while their parents were away on the weekends for one of their dates. On rare instances, when Nell was able to leave her jobs early or if they were cancelled, she would sneak away to a nearby ice cream shop, treating herself to something inexpensive from the menu like a soda or a scoop of ice cream. She enjoyed observing people socialize with one another and how excited they would be to get a delectable treat, taking moments to appreciate the simple things in life. Nell's eyes lit up at the sight of how excited the small children would be to enter the shop, pulling their parents inside to buy them sweets. Nell smiled at the sight of two teens enjoying what seemed to be a date between two people who were loving each other's company. The two were drinking their chocolate milkshakes and having a fun conversation amongst themselves. The guy was listening attentively with a wide smile and his date was eagerly informing him of a hilarious situation that happened to her earlier that day.

I hope that moment is one that they both will treasure, Nell thought, taking a sip of her soda.

Chapter 18

Squeezing between a pair of children running down the hallway, Nell opened the door to her parents' apartment. She was exhausted and her feet ached. She had spent the day with the Williams twins, and they had been extra active, running around the house, pretending to be characters from a television show.

Mr. Jefferson sat on the sofa, also fatigued from working his construction job over the weekday as a painter and painting homes for individual homeowners who hired him for extra income during the weekends. Nell's sister and brother were sitting at the kitchen table with their books opened, working on their given assignments from Mr. and Mrs. Jefferson each summer, as Nell used to, under her parents' guidance.

Nell's six-year-old brother, George turned his head.

"May I go to Cornelius' house?" the boy asked Mrs. Jefferson, who was reading an article from a woman's magazine in the living room that was across from the kitchen.

"Did you finish your work?" Mrs. Jefferson asked.

"Yes, ma'am."

"Let me see it."

The boy gathered his papers, handing them to his mother. Mrs. Jefferson studied the answers.

"You forgot to do the second row," she told him, giving him back his paper.

George rushed back to the table, working on the missed parts of his paper. Nell walked past him, stopping at the kitchen counter. She spotted the new black cultural magazine, sparking an interest. Sitting next to her siblings, she began browsing through it. George peeked nearby.

"Ma," he called out. "I want to read the magazine too."

"Boy, didn't I tell you to finish those math problems?" Mrs. Jefferson called out back to him from the other room.

Nell smirked, recalling how tough her parents used to be with her for years. She used to be annoyed with her parents making her read books, do math, and other subjects during the summer. They made her and her siblings do it for as long as she could remember. By the time Nell was older, tasks like those became a breeze, resulting in her finishing earlier. The only subject she struggled in was math. What used to be so easy became difficult with the complexity of the different equations. Nell missed those days, going to school and learning different subjects. What had become a chore had become a pleasant memory, the more she thought about it.

They are so lucky, Nell thought about her siblings. *I wish that I hadn't taken those days for granted. To sit back and learn something for the heck of it. Yeah, mom and dad can be tough, but they mean well.*

Closing her book, Claudine, Nell's sixteen-year-old sister, went to the kitchen counter and began rummaging through the mail. Most of the mail were letters for Mr. and Mrs. Jefferson, but one was addressed to her from Wood Oak, Louisiana. A grin slowly crept upon her face. She began to giggle, alerting her siblings who began to stare at her suspiciously.

George tossed his pencil on the table and handed his mother his paper again. Agreeing with his completed answers, he was free from his required tasks. Nonchalantly, he crept next to Claudine who was now opening her treasured letter, placing the envelope on the kitchen counter, and reading the letter within. George picked up the envelope, piercing his lip and widening his eyes next to his unsuspecting sister.

"Oooh," he cried out, waving the envelope. "Pa! Look!"

Mr. Jefferson's eyes remained closed, rubbing his temples.

"Not, now, son," he answered. "I have a headache."

"Claudine has a boyfriend!" George blurted out, making Mr. Jefferson's eyes shoot open, turning to his youngest daughter. Everyone turned Claudine's way. Claudine's mouth dropped open, shooting her brother an angry squint.

"What *boyfriend*?" Mr. Jefferson demanded, giving his daughter an equally enraged glimpse.

Claudine crumbled the letter in her hands, hiding it between herself and the countertop. With her free hand, she shoved her brother on the top of his head. George shoved her back, attempting to also snatch the crumbled letter between his sister and the counter.

"I don't have a boyfriend," Claudine argued, snapping her lips at her brother.

"Look," George rushed to Mr. Jefferson, handing him the envelope. Smirking impishly, he began to laugh at the increased fury his father was beginning to have with his eyes.

"*Tyrone Parker*," Mr. Jefferson read out loud from the envelope. "Isn't he Evelyn's boy?"

"Yeah," Mrs. Jefferson said, her voice straining at the recollection. "He has an older brother. I forgot what his name was. The one that used to have a thing for Nell...Marlon....Melvin...no, Martin!"

"Why is *Tyrone* writing to *you* letters, Claudine?" Mr. Jefferson demanded. "You know you're not allowed to date!"

"We aren't dating each other," Claudine contended. "We used to do projects together in class and kept on touch. He's not the only person I write to. I write to a girl named Darla Carpenter. We were classmates, that's all."

"Maybe you should have left all contact with the *boy* in Wood Oak," Mr. Jefferson said dryly.

"*He's in Wood Oak*," Claudine reminded them. "It's not even a love letter! He only wrote to tell me that a lot of places in Wood Oak were closing, including Sal's Country Store."

"Serves them right," Mr. Jefferson muttered, closing his eyes once again. "I wish they had less time to pack like we did. That rushed move nearly killed me."

"It's not too bad in Illinois," Mrs. Jefferson added. "It's been easier to find work here and there is more to do."

"True," Mr. Jefferson agreed. "But it's not the same. Its warmer down south and the gumbo that used to be served at Brian's Seafood was my favorite food. Name one place here that comes even close to food back home."

"Their dirty rice was really good," Nell chimed in. "They put something in that seasoning that makes it taste better than any I ever had."

"The crawfish etouffee was my favorite," Mrs. Jefferson sighed. "The one at Peabody's Cafeteria is close, but theirs is a too diluted."

"I liked their jello," said George.

"You can get jello anywhere," Claudine groaned. "You ate some yesterday!"

"It didn't have any whipped cream on it."

"Then put it on yourself!"

"You two better stop all that bickering," Mrs. Jefferson said eyeballing her squabbling children with "the look."

"I was talking to Mr. Butler who teaches at the community college," Mr. Jefferson informed the family. "He said he works a second job at the night school. Nell is going to finish her education, after she has the baby."

Nell did a double take. Her hand rushed towards her mouth to cover it. *School? Did he just say that I could finish? Even after having the baby? He didn't give up on me after all!*

"What about working?" Nell questioned her father.

"You can still work part-time," Mr. Jefferson suggested. "I took time from work to enroll you in classes next year so you can finish school and get that high school diploma. It took a while for us to get your high school transcripts from Wood Oak High School, but we got them and now you can be back on track with your education. This is your second chance; don't ruin it."

"And I can watch the baby in the evenings," Mrs. Jefferson added.

"So can I," Claudine offered.

"Me too," George squealed.

"Thank you," Nell said, rejuvenated by enthusiasm.

Chapter 19

For the next few days, Nell did her duties taking care of Mrs. Betty and the Williams brothers. Miraculously, she convinced her parents to allow her to go to the library when she had free time. There, Nell began reading the science and math books, hoping to refresh her scholastic memories. She would sit in the far back of the library, cramming until it was time to go.

I will not make the same mistakes again, she thought. *Besides taking care of my baby, school is going to be one of my top priorities. I can still be the first in my family to graduate from high school. I will make my parents proud.*

Hours later, exiting the library, Nell walked a few blocks, turning into the street where her family lived. The streets were busy with people coming and going, narrowing the walking path. Nell clutched tightly to the notebook she had been carrying with her. In the notebook, she wrote down notes and different formulas, eager to study them when she returned home. Today, she had at least ten pages filled that she was going to review again that evening. No matter what, she was determined to make sure that her second chance was not in vain.

Nell strolled into the family's apartment building, collecting the daily mail. Climbing up the stairs, she scanned the new magazines and fliers. There were tons of mail that day, including another letter to Claudine, this time from Darla Carpenter from Wood Oak, Louisiana. There were bills addressed to her parents, making her feel guilty. Months ago, Nell offered them portions of her earnings to help with the debts, but her parents refused. They simply stated that they wanted her to keep her earnings to buy diapers and other necessities for later. As an alternative, Nell did more around the apartment such as cooking tasks, if she got home before everyone else, which included that day.

Placing the piles of mail onto the kitchen counter, Nell began prepping for dinner. She washed her hands and began cutting onions, garlic, and other items for the smothered porkchops that the family would be eating that evening. Nell learned a lot from staying with Mrs. Ann back in Magnolia, Louisiana. Mrs. Ann had taught her the recipe that she was using, and it was amongst one of the best meals Nell had ever eaten. She hoped that once her family took their first bite, that they would love it just as much as she did when she first tasted the meal.

While the pork was cooking, Nell began rummaging through the mail again. More advertisements, junk mail, a letter for Mr. Jefferson from her Uncle Walter in Michigan, and lastly, a letter addressed to her from Paul Boudreaux in South Carolina.

Nell's mouth dropped, freezing. Taking a shaky breath, Nell leaned against the kitchen counter. Almost hyperventilating, she clutched onto the envelope while she ambled to a nearby chair, sitting down. Teary eyed, she opened the envelope to read the letter inside:

Babe,

I apologize for leaving earlier than expected in Louisiana and not contacting you sooner. I wanted to be there with you to see you be reunited with your family in Illinois, but my uncle sent for me before I could go with you and Henry. For the last few months, my Uncle Simon had me placed in a private military academy in Alabama where I was able to finish the remainder of my senior year of high school. The school was as stringent as all get out, but I made it through.

Since I turned eighteen and completed school, he isn't so adamant about me "embarrassing and disappointing" him and my deceased parents. Right now, I am in recruit training at the Marine Corp Recruit Depot in South Carolina.

I tried to find you, but Henry had the paper that had your address and phone number. I called Mr. Holiday, but Henry was gone for a long time. Apparently, he was searching for me, gave up, and went back to Florida to stay with his folks there for a bit. He eventually contacted Mr. Holiday, who told him that I was looking for him and we were able to reconnect. He still had the

paper with the contact information, and I was able to work from there. I tried calling the number several times, but never got an answer or the phone line would be busy, so I'm writing this letter instead. I hope this address is still current! I want you to know that I haven't forgotten about you and miss you. Nell, if this is a good address, and I'm hoping that it is, do me the honor of writing back. I'd like to know if there is still a chance that you would take me back as your boyfriend or as much, give me the opportunity to be in your life in some way and our baby's life once he or she is born. I love you and always will.

Paul

Chapter 20

"So, what is it going to be?" Mr. Jefferson questioned Nell that evening.

The entire household was hushed, including Claudine and George who were asked to go into the back bedroom that Nell shared with her sister. Nell was in the living room with her parents. Mr. Jefferson was seated in his lounge chair staring at her with the most resentment she had seen in a long time from him. Mrs. Jefferson's head hung low, shaking it slowly from side to side, eyes closed. Nell made no attempts to wipe her loose tears away from her face.

"You going to go run back to that white boy again?" Mr. Jefferson asked Nell. "After everything that this household had gone through because of your relationship with him! We are *not* going to be caught up in all that mess for a second time."

"But I love him and we're expecting a baby together," Nell sobbed. "Paul isn't this awful person you think he is! He didn't kick anyone out of Wood Oak!"

"You better get some sense and cut him loose," Mr. Jefferson warned her, "We've already agreed to help you raise the baby, but you are not allowed to be with that white boy, you hear me! You either follow my rules while you are living under my roof, or you can just pack your bags and go be with him!"

Nell shot her father a long, pained look before breaking eye contact.

"Paul cares about me and the baby," Nell argued, her chin trembling. "He wouldn't have written this letter if he didn't!"

"He got his diploma," Mr. Jefferson bellowed. "What do you have? Nothing except his baby that he will probably abandon too once another cute little thing comes his way. You want to be on welfare like all the other girls who have nothing because they were too stupid to not keep their legs closed? It's either him or us! You better choose wisely because once you leave, don't think of ever coming back!"

Her body quaking, Nell wiped the tears away from her face. Rising to her feet, she stormed out of the living room and into the bedroom that she shared with Claudine. Claudine was sitting in her bed with her legs tucked towards her with her arms wrapped around them. She had tears running down her face. Unwrapping her legs, she rushed towards Nell who began going through the dresser, stuffing clothes into a bag. Her hands had a slight tremble, rushing.

"Nell," Claudine cried out, "don't go. We all want you to stay!" She grabbed at one of the shirts that Nell had in her hands and began pulling it towards herself. Irate, Nell jerked the shirt back, ripping it out of her sister's hands.

George ran outside the room, his face sorrowful. He rushed to his mother, crying.

"I don't want Nell to go," he wept. He cried out a long wail, while his mother held onto him, tears also pouring down her face.

With her bag stuffed, Nell stormed out of the apartment and into the streets.

Chapter 21

Paul

"Forward march," Drill Instructor Dallas ordered. He stood tall in his squared away uniform, his campaign hat or in other words, his "smokey the bear hat," and his spit-shined boots. His voice was deep, booming, and one of the highest authorities on the field as the senior drill instructor. Beads of sweat began to form on his forehead from the torturous, blazing sun. The next two powers of authority were the two junior drill instructors: Drill Instructor Payne and Drill Instructor Keller, both just as brutal as the senior drill instructor, showing no pity for the weak and those who were dumb enough to attempt to test their power. Mercy was neither given by the sky that had no clouds that torrid day in South Carolina. Used to the sweltering sun, most southern men had no complaints about the heat and those that did knew it was best to keep their mouths shut.

It was a few days into basic training, and it was the recruits' third attempt to march in unison that day. The men hadn't gone ten feet without someone tripping over their own two feet, resulting in the recruits having to start over once again on the drill field. A recruit named Justin Tillman made an incorrect facing movement by moving his body to the left when it was called to be a right facing movement. His error was noted by Drill Instructor Dallas, who instructed for the entire platoon to restart once again, after calling them a bunch of "dumbasses" or "stooges."

"Private, do you know your left from your right?" Drill Instructor Dallas shouted at Justin. "Your *other* right!"

"Yes, sir," Justin responded.

"All you scumbags, start again," Drill Instructor Dallas commanded.

All the men hurried to start the process over again, until it was done correctly and to the drill instructor's standards.

As frightening as things were in recruit training, eighteen-year-old, Paul Boudreaux was glad to be there, conditioning his body to go above and beyond its usual limits. With each verbal assault, he mentally encouraged himself to succeed and to be an even better active listener than before, focusing on complying to the orders of the drill instructors. His heart throb signature jet black hair was shaven days ago, leaving a "high and tight" style. His grey eyes were alert and eager. The training's morning formations and drills reminded him of being out on the field with his former high school's football team, doing their regular drills, only the marine corps was stricter and allowed no room for error. Anything that was not perfected was done over repeatedly until it was.

I wonder how Nell is doing and if she had received my letter yet, Paul thought. *She should be due in two months, and I need to contact her and her family to see if they will give me permission to marry her.*

"Fall out," Drill Instructor Dallas directed as the recruits lined in the same order as before. "Left face…Right face…Dammit Henderson! I said to the right! Don't you know your right from your left?! Everyone, start again!"

The recruits were exhausted but did not complain. Once more, they redid the drill until it was done correctly. The day was long and exhausting, but eventually the new recruits succeeded.

Dinner time faired no different; it was equally strict and quiet in the Mess Hall. The day's meal included: meatloaf, mashed potatoes and gravy, carrots, and milk. Meatloaf was Paul's favorite meal, but he knew better than to dive in and eat. He placed his tray down on the table and stood behind it. Other recruits did the same, as trained. Drill Instructor Payne stood near, waiting for the last recruit to stand in place. With all men accounted for, it was time to await the next order.

"Ready; seat," Drill Instructor Payne instructed. "Commence eating! No talking!"

Paul and the rest of the recruits sat down and began to quietly eat their meal. *It's hilarious that they aren't telling us to chew together in unison,* Paul thought.

Days later, the recruits followed the same routine daily: leaving the two-story wooden barracks from their bunk beds, go to breakfast, then go to their classes which composed of military subjects such as the history of the marine corps, squad techniques, rifle repair, with each class lasting forty-five minutes, and lastly, close order drill on the parade deck, which was also known as "the grinder." After classes, the men would go to lunch and then fall into formation and march some more. The day was the same with the routines, formations, physical training, and on rare occasion, goof-ups.

Sometimes the goof-ups would result in the men scrubbing the floors with toothbrushes, doing extra drills on the drill field, or completing "as many pushups as there were in the world." One day, Drill Instructor Dallas gawked at the men during a drill.

"You recruits look like a bunch of cattle," he barked. "While you all are marching say 'mooo'! Everyone better be mooing!"

"Mooo!" the recruits roared.

Drill Instructor Dallas turned to the hatch man of the platoon, and said, "Hatch man, run ahead and say, 'Sir, the barn door is open, and the drill instructor can let the herd in.'"

The hatch man sprinted ahead of the platoon. As ordered, he opened the doors to barracks and replied,

"Sir, the barn door is open, and the drill instructor can let the herd in."

"Everyone 'moo' until you get inside the door," Drill Instructor Dallas said.

"Moo!" the recruits echoed, entering the barracks.

Inside the building, the men now began their free time to clean their rifles, wash their clothes with a scrub brush to hang out to dry on the side of their beds, and polish their brass, boots, and shoes. After that was completed, some decided to stretch out near their footlockers and began talks of cars, food, drills, girls, and their futures. Others went to the showers, brushed their teeth, or used the bathroom.

"I wish I had a nice big juicy burger right now," a recruit named Timothy Blythe said, polishing his belt. "My girl and I used to go to this burger joint back in Orlando, Florida and they had the juiciest burgers of all time. I can smell and picture it all right now. Imagine all that cheese oozing on the size mixed with the beef juices, soaking up in a thick bun with extra thick tomato and mayonnaise."

"Just give me a nice stack of pancakes smothered in syrup and I will be in heaven," Justin Tillman replied.

"Good thing they already make my favorite here: meatloaf," Paul boasted, laughing.

"Enjoy it while you still can, you may not have it next time where you have orders to," Timothy said, smirking.

During mail call, Paul waited to see if any of his letters would be from Nell, but none came from her, dampening his spirits. Uncertain of the validity of the address given to him by Henry, Paul considered expanding his search, using different addresses, but with a new military career, he had limited time to plan such a task.

"You want to hear something crazy," Justin said, sitting on his bunk.

"What?" Timothy asked.

"My brother received a draft notice while serving in Vietnam," Justin laughed. "He told his first sergeant that he needed to return to the United States, or he would go to jail."

"Really? Did they send him back?"

"No, his first sergeant had to send a letter to the Headquarters of the Marine Corp saying he was already serving."

An hour later, Paul turned to the clock that hung on the wall.

"Guys, it's almost that time," Paul informed them, his eyes shifting away.

The recruits quickly put away their belongings and Drill Instructor Keller went in and told them to put everything up and prepare for TAPS (signal to turn out the lights and go to bed). The men put their belongings away and stood next to their bunks.

"Prepare to mount," Drill Instructor Keller ordered. "Mount."

The men got into their bunks and lied down at attention.

"Lights out," Drill Instructor Keller said. He turned off the lights and exited the barracks. Soon after, the recruits got under the covers and went to sleep.

For a total of thirteen weeks, the men trained in South Carolina until it was time to graduate. After the graduation ceremony, Paul scanned the bleachers from the parade deck, not seeing the face he wanted to see the most. His eyes saddened; Paul stared out to the parade deck where the other families had gathered. Amongst them, was his Uncle Simon, talking to one of the military retirees. Nearby, Paul saw his friend, Henry approaching him. He made it to the graduation, but unfortunately, he didn't make it into the buddy system with Paul due to him being in a different state when Paul's uncle made him sign up for selective service. However, once Henry turned eighteen, he enlisted to follow in Paul's footsteps. The friends began to talk, catching up on old times, and their goals for the future.

Chapter 22

After graduating from recruit training, Paul spent the next few weeks in infantry training learning to be a skilled ground pounder. Afterwards, he was assigned to his artillery unit to become a Field Artillery Battery Man in North Carolina. This meant that he and the men in his unit would oversee shooting, cleaning, and repairing cannons (155-millimeter howitzers). Soon, Paul was given orders from his first sergeant in the battery office that he would be deployed to Vietnam, a place Paul had never been to before.

Where in the heck is that place, Paul wondered, taking his papers.

Paul was flown to California where he received a four-hour orientation on where he was going next: Okinawa for two weeks to get his medical shots, receive his gear for combat, receive an additional orientation to where he was going, and be assigned to his Vietnam unit. Later, he boarded a plane and was flown to a military base in Vietnam. There, military personnel took him to his assigned unit. Paul, like many men who accompanied him, had one wish: to not get shot. In their assigned compound, Paul's unit spent many days filling sandbags. The sandbags would later be used to help put different guns into position and to protect the guns from the bullets, hence, creating a barrier. Other duties included supporting neighboring compounds that were a distance away from Paul's assigned compound. In a routine, most of the day was spent leaving the compound to go a mile, fire rounds (guns) to support another unit with artillery, pick up, and return to their own compound.

One day, after a daunting day of gunfire, the realities of his chances of not coming home began to run through Paul's mind. Still, he persisted, taking one day at a time.

Days later, Paul received a letter from his childhood friend, Henry Wilkerson. Paul opened it and began to read.

Paul,

How are you, pal? Things are fine here; just surviving day to day. I will spare you the details of reading about how frustrating it is to not eat some good old southern cooking from back home.

I got some bad news for you. I got a letter from Stephen back in Wood Oak about your family. Our fathers still talk, so that's how he was able to keep in touch with me. He wrote that your cousin, Wally, went to his father to get legal advice on taking over all your properties there, including Sal's. Also, he's been having garage sales, selling off your belongings, including your old car. Wally's been staying in your grandfather's house the entire time you've been gone but wants to legally

take over the other houses to sell and make profits. I guess he figured that since you've been gone for a while that you wouldn't go back to Wood Oak. During the garage sales, Stephen got your old letterman jacket and a few books that had some family pictures, but he said that those were dumped in the trashcan by Wally, who still wanted to sell them for money when Stephen wanted to take them. Unfortunately, most of the photos were cut up or scratched out. Stephen said that he's talked to his father about you never giving up those items, but they need proof that what Wally is doing is illegal. Otherwise, it's Stephen's word against Wally's who is telling everyone you gave everything to him. Stephen said that whatever he managed to save, he wants to give back to you, but I don't know which address you'd want me to give him to use to give you back your stuff.

Also, Bill, your other cousin, is still living at his parents' house, but nobody has seen his father in a while and there is no telling what happened to him. Bill barely graduated from the high school, but is still seeing your old girlfriend, Nancy. He's supposedly working for some construction company since Sal's shut down. If I were you, I'd do something fast before your relatives do more damage. I can see why your grandfather didn't want to leave them anything and it's becoming more apparent to everyone in The Family that they went after the wrong person, despite them resenting you for being with Nell and knowing how manipulative your relatives can be. I

wish I had better news for you, but you should be aware of what is going on in your absence.

Henry

Paul's body tensed as the heat flushed through his body. His face turned red as he began to imagine himself pounding Wally to a pulp.

How dare he, Paul thought, thinking about his cousin, Wally. *He really didn't care about anybody but himself! It wasn't enough that he successfully turned almost everyone in Wood Oak against me and Nell, almost getting us killed because of his greed! Even after I offered to split everything equally before all this crap went down! It's because of him that Nell and I couldn't finish high school there and were forced to flee with just the clothes on our backs! Over my dead body if he thinks he will get a cent more of any money or properties that were willed to me!*

Furious, Paul rose from his seat to speak to his first sergeant about contacting JAG (Judge Advocate Generals) and his parents' trustee, his uncle, Simon.

Days later, Paul signed the documents provided to him by the JAG attorney to remove Wally and any other relatives from the properties left to him by his grandfather and parents.

Chapter 23

Paul, 1972- 1974

Two years after Paul's active-duty deployment, he was allowed to return to the states, with four years of reserve duty. He worried about his estates, but his uncle and attorneys assured him that his Wood Oak relatives were gone from each of his properties and that each home and business was boarded up. Simon informed Paul that he took it upon himself to hire people to check on the properties, while he himself went there every two weeks to check on his sister's grave. With that settled, Paul went back to Alabama to focus more on his scholastic career, still wanting to fulfill his dream of being a high school coach and possibly a businessman, like his father. Paul successfully enrolled into a private Alabama university in 1973 double majoring in business and education. For a year, his campus life had been a serious one, focusing mainly on his studies.

It was not until the spring of 1974 that he even took the time to even consider dating again. Returning to his short heartthrob hairstyle, Paul was still a young and attractive man, turning twenty-two in a few months, but had been unable to maintain any relationship once things were beginning to become serious.

"Why?" the girls would sob. "I thought that things were going well for us. What did I do?"

"Nothing," Paul would say. "It's not you, it's me." Ending each relationship, he would simply walk away, his heart refusing to invest any further. Reaching into his pants pocket, he would still carry the treasured handkerchief, caressing it with his fingers. The days of him crying over the girl who made it for him had long passed. There were no more tears left to cry, but it continued to haunt and cloud his heart and mind.

Chapter 24

"Why don't you just get the operator to call her old address," Paul's friend suggested over the phone, after hearing why Paul wouldn't date his sister.

"I did that years ago," Paul replied, staring at the sky from the phone booth and watching the clouds move by. "The last time I called, the person who answered told me that the Jeffersons had moved, but nobody knows where to. I'm a father and I don't even know if I have a son or a daughter. I can't even bring myself to be around little kids without thinking about the one I never had the opportunity to hold and raise. That sounds crazy, huh. I bet if I ran into my old girlfriend, she'd never forgive me for not being there for the birth. I haven't forgiven myself."

"It's not your fault. How can you be a father to your kid when nobody knows where they are?"

Tap! Tap!

Paul lowered his gaze, trying hard not to grumble. A girl named Cindy Spearman was tapping on the window to get his attention. She was a twenty-year-old art major with blonde hair and brown eyes wearing a solid brown dress and white shoes. She reminded Paul a lot of his old girlfriend, Nancy Perkins. After going on a few dates, she was eager to be Paul's girl, ready to take the relationship to the next level. That is, until Paul ended the relationship days ago.

"I gotta go," Paul said to his friend. "I'll talk to you later, buddy." He hung up the phone and exited the booth, giving Cindy an annoyed stare that she ignored.

"Hey, Paul," Cindy said, running her fingers through her long blonde hair. "I know that we broke up, but I was hoping that we could still be friends and hang out as we did before."

"Thanks, but I'm not interested in doing that," Paul replied. "I have too much to do with my classes. I don't want a serious relationship with anyone, and I know that's what you want. Neither of us should waste the other's time."

Before he knew it, Cindy kissed him. She parted her lips to deepen the kiss, but Paul turned his head.

"You always have that sad look on your face," Cindy said. "We don't have to have anything serious, if you don't want to. We can have fun and enjoy ourselves, even if its temporary. We wouldn't be wasting each other's time, if it's something we both can benefit from. It'll feel good and you'll be less stressed."

"I don't know," Paul said, after a long pause. "Are you sure you want to do that? We really don't have to. To be honest, that won't change anything."

Grabbing Paul's hand, Cindy pulled him into one of the university buildings. A few students were walking down the hallway or leaving. Entering a less crowded pathway, Cindy opened the door to an empty classroom, tugging at Paul's hand to follow her inside. Closing the door behind them, Cindy turned to Paul, kissing him. Paul stood there, staring at the classroom walls. He caught whiff of Cindy's perfume averting his eyes towards her.

She does smell nice, Paul thought. *But...I am not sure that I want this, with her. What's wrong with me? I used to like making out with girls, but why does it still hurt all the same whenever someone tries to get closer? I should just leave.*

Cindy's hands trailed down. She paused, looking down, noticing the handkerchief that was partially sticking out. Cindy grabbed it, pulling it out. Nonchalantly, she dropped it into the wastebasket before reaching for Paul's belt buckle.

Reddening in the face, Paul grabbed Cindy's hand, shoving it away. Cindy let out a surprised gasp, rapidly blinking as she tried to process what had happened. His eyes turning cold at the mere sight of Cindy, Paul retrieved the cloth from the wastebasket. He shoved the handkerchief back into his pocket before opening the door and storming out of the room.

"W-wait," Cindy called out, following Paul out of the building. "What's wrong? What did I do *this* time?"

Paul jammed his hands in his pockets, continuing his retreat until Cindy touched his shoulder that he jerked away.

"Get lost," Paul snapped at her, shooting her a cold, hard look.

"Why do you have to be like this?" Cindy demanded. "You're upset with me over some ugly old rag!"

Paul's body tensed; his eyes narrowed at her with an ugly twist to his mouth.

"Yes," he agreed, his tone deepening. "That handkerchief that you called an 'ugly old rag' means more to me than you ever will. Do me a favor, next time we run into each other, keep walking."

A tightness in his eyes, Paul went away to his new blue car that was purchased a few weeks ago. Due to the trust funds left to him by his parents and grandfather, he was allowed to have a monthly allowance of one thousand dollars until he turned twenty-five years old. At the age of twenty-five, Paul would be allowed to manage his own inheritance and properties completely on his own. Until then, his uncle, Simon, was his trustee who managed his affairs.

Returning home to his off-campus apartment, Paul shut the door behind himself and turned on the television set. Of course, nothing was on that he cared to watch, but he needed a distraction. Cindy worked his last nerve, just like the other girls that he had been dating. It would have been easy to just have sex with each girl, but then that would probably mean they would come back worse than ever. Paul wasn't sure himself what he wanted. Everything was a complete mind jumble, and he needed his mind clear for his classes at the very least. He was too upset to concentrate on anything. Most of his days were like that when it came to dating. Just when things were looking better, something, even the tiniest thing, would upset him.

Knock! Knock!

Swearing under his breath and slamming his fist against the armrest of the couch, Paul rose to his feet, opening the door to his apartment. Outside stood Cindy, her face distraught and mouth downturned.

"I'm sorry," she said. "I didn't mean to offend you by what I said. It will never happen again; you have my word. I don't want things to end this way between us. Give me one more chance to make things up to you."

"Didn't I tell you to get lost?"

Cindy broke down into a heavy sob. Her mascara began to run down her cheeks. Her posture bent as she clutched her shirt with her hand.

Paul grabbed the door handle to slam the door in Cindy's face, but something that was buried deep within him resurfaced, remembering the sobs of another from a long time ago. For that moment, Paul could see *her* face again, sitting next to him in the car crying hysterically as he sat nearby. *I… I'm so sorry; forgive me…*Regretful, Paul's icy eyes and heart softened, looking upon Cindy who was also crying. *What kind of person have I become? Each day, I'm becoming more of a stranger to everyone, including myself.*

"I'm sorry," Paul said, pausing at the door. "I don't mean to be this horrible guy, but I have a lot going on in my life that I am struggling to cope with. I'm working on trying to be kinder to people, but it's been tough these last few years after losing someone I wanted to be with for the rest of my life."

"That's okay, Paul," Cindy told him, steadily calming down and straightening her stance. "I understand. Earlier, I wanted to invite you to join me and a few friends at the movie theater. We all usually hang out in the dorms afterwards to hang out and listen to music. You want to join?"

Rubbing his hands through his hair, Paul wondered what he should do. He wanted to say no, but he figured that if he wanted to work on himself, he would have to work on not snapping at people.

"Okay," Paul stated, "Again, sorry about earlier. I was being a jerk and shouldn't have been so harsh. Going to the movies sounds great. When and which movie theater?"

"8 o'clock at the Star Gazer Movie Theater," Cindy said.

"I'll pick you up at 7:45 p.m.," Paul replied.

"Great," Cindy said. Turning away, she left the apartment complex, awaiting their time at movies.

Chapter 25

The audience roared with laughter. It was the night of the movie and Paul was having a wonderful time with Cindy and her friends. They were watching a romantic comedy and it was better than Paul had anticipated. Cindy wasn't the insensitive girl he expected her to be after the whole handkerchief incident. She was outgoing and flirtatious, like he used to be. Cindy took it upon herself to hold his hand and rest her head upon his shoulder. It felt nice to Paul, to have someone think so much of him to not give up on him as he had done so many times. For years, he tried to bury his past with his military duties and school. It was nice to be a step closer to finding the happiness he yearned for.

Cindy grinned at Paul, her eyes longing. Paul smiled, leaning down and giving her a quick smooch, feeling better about himself and the direction that things were going. He let out a soft muffled moan when Cindy returned the kiss, deepening it the way Paul liked.

"Let's say you and I sneak out of here," Cindy flirted in a whisper, giving Paul a wink.

"Or it would be more fun if we stayed," Paul teased, chuckling at thoughts of a public make out session.

"You'd like that, huh," Cindy giggled.

"Yeah," Paul flirted, his smile widening.

They were sitting in the back row and the other patrons were either watching the movie or engaged in their own make out sessions.

With only a piece of fabric from Paul's shirt between them, Cindy caressed Paul's abs with the tip of her finger. It felt nice and Paul was beginning to feel good, wanting more. He nodded his head towards the exit. Beaming, Cindy and Paul left the room that the movie was showing. They strolled along the theater, searching for a place, but where? They both entered the men's restroom. Paul locked the door, lifting Cindy and sitting her on top of the counter where the sinks were. Continuing their make out session, their bodies became flushed. Cindy lifted her shirt above her head, removing it, and revealing her bra.

Boom! Boom! Boom! The loud strikes to the locked door sounded.

"Hey," a voice on the other side of the door cried out. "Why is this door locked?"

Paul and Cindy paused their kissing session, squinted their eyes at the door. Then, unexpectantly, a toilet from one of the stalls flushed, further surprising the couple. Swearing under her breath, Cindy began to redress when the stall door flew open.

"Whoa, alright," exclaimed a young teen who was exiting the stall. He was all smiles seeing Cindy's bra before she covered it with her shirt.

Cindy leapt from the counter, standing behind Paul to hide her shamed face. Paul tossed his head back, mortified. The teen smirked approaching the sink to wash his hands.

Boom! Boom! Boom!

"Let me in," the voice on the other side of the door begged. "I need to go *now!*"

Annoyed, Paul unlocked the bathroom door, letting in a desperate man who dashed into the bathroom. The man didn't care to question why a woman was in there. The man flew open the bathroom stall door, slamming it shut. Right away, the man let out an explosive fart, forcing Paul, Cindy, and the other teen to make disgusted faces. The plopping sounds of excrement falling into the toilet between the farts made Cindy gag, hurrying out to leave the disgusting scene with Paul and the other teen not too far from behind her.

Cindy rushed to a nearby wall, closing her eyes and pressing the palm of her hand against her chest. Her face was appalled.

"You think you can get her to show her bra again?" the teen from the bathroom inquired.

"Get out of here, kid," Paul said, his voice on edge.

Cindy's friends and the movie crowd exited the room that the movie was playing in. People shot them confused looks seeing Cindy in distress with Paul inches away from her. Backing his hands in a surrender position, Paul shook his head. Movie night had ended.

Chapter 26

Weeks later with his tests completed, it was time for spring break and Paul decided to spend most of his time with Cindy and her friends, who became his. They began to hang out at the parks, restaurants, or each other's apartments to chat, listen to the new songs on records, or watch movies. All was going well with Paul considering the possibility of going steady with Cindy. They talked daily, and slowly; she was beginning to unlock Paul's frozen heart.

Over the phone, Cindy asked him if she could spend the night at his place, wanting to take their blossoming relationship to another level.

"Sure, why not," Paul said contemplating the idea.

"And Paul," Cindy added. "I know it's early to be telling you this, but, I love you."

Her words hit Paul like a ton of bricks, making him do a double take, unsure as to how to respond. It had been years since Paul had uttered those words to anyone. The pain associated with them began to resurface, making Paul nauseous and dizzy. He swallowed hard, unable to articulate them back.

"I...I'll see you tonight," Paul said, feeling guilty afterwards. He hung up the phone. His body crumpled in on itself. There was a pain in the back of his throat that he tried to clear when there was a knock at the door. Rising to his feet, Paul was stunned to see a police officer and a well-dressed man in a suit standing on the other side when he opened it. Paul's mouth got dry, taking in a deep breath to calm himself.

A police officer, he thought. *Oh crap! What is going on now?*

"Mr. Boudreaux," the man in the suit addressed him, "I'm Mr. Everson and I am a lawyer from the Everson Law Firm. He is Officer Fredrickson." He extended his hand. Reluctantly, Paul shook it. "Mr. Boudreaux, this letter came in the mail for you, and we were wondering if you'll accept it." Mr. Everson forwarded a letter to Paul with his free hand.

His stomach churning, Paul took the letter, studying it. It was a letter that had been stamped so many times, that there was barely any room left. The letter was sent multiple times to numerous states, Japan, Vietnam, and always returning to his first address and ended in his current address. It was addressed to him from almost four years ago from Nell Jefferson.

Babe, Paul's heart sunk so much that he almost collapsed to the floor. Leaning against the door frame, he pushed back the tears that began to brim upon his eyes.

"Mr. Boudreaux," Mr. Everson repeated, "are you willing to accept the letter?"

"Yes," Paul said, choking back a sob. "Do I need to sign for it?"

"No, sir, have a wonderful day," Mr. Everson told him, turning around to leave.

"I just wanted to see what would happen, out of curiosity," the officer confessed, grinning and turning around to follow the lawyer.

His hands shaking, Paul opened the letter, wiping away the tears that were beginning to flow heavily.

Paul,

I received your letter a few days ago and I wanted to write back to tell you, yes! I most definitely want to still be your girlfriend, more than anything! Thanks for remembering, caring, and not giving up on me when it seems like everyone else always is. You truly are my biggest support and I love you!

I tried to go to the South Carolina address you had on the envelope to see you but wasn't allowed. So, I'm sending you this letter instead, and I hope you receive it and write back to me soon using my current address on the envelope. I don't have much money on me, so I'm going to be staying at the Rose Baptist Church on 9th Street in Rose, South Carolina for as long as I can. They

are one of the few places where I could go for a place to stay with limited resources. I will write again soon!

Love always,

Nell

"Write again?" Paul shouted, *"Again?* Then where are my other letters?"

Rushing to his phone with a tightness in his chest, Paul dialed for the operator, asking to connect him to the Rose Baptist Church on 9th Street in Rose, South Carolina. *You did write back! Nell, I didn't know! What happened? Where are you?*

"Hello," a tired feminine voice answered after being connected to Paul. "Rose Baptist Church…"

"This is Paul Boudreaux," Paul said, his voice rushed. "I'm looking for Nell Jefferson. She was seventeen and pregnant at the time. She wrote a letter to me almost four years ago, but I'm just now receiving it. Please, tell me, do you know where she is?"

"Sir," the woman said, "I'm going to have to ask you to repeat what you just said and say it slowly because I could barely understand a word."

Eagerly, his heart racing, Paul repeated himself, his voice shaking.

"Yeah," the woman answered, as if recollecting. "We sometimes have young mothers come in. I think Nell was one of the ones who didn't want to put her baby girl up for adoption. She was sweet but left us weeks after having her daughter. She left with this other young mother, but I don't know where they went after they left us, but someone found letters Nell wrote that didn't get mailed. I assume she gave them to Martha, but Martha's mind was slipping, and we often must make sure she sends the church letters out. Sometimes things slip through the cracks."

How the heck could you miss such important letters, Paul wanted to shout through the phone. *You should have mailed them!*

"Where are the letters?" Paul asked. "Were they addressed to me?"

"I don't know," the lady admitted. "The reverend had them in his office the last time I saw them, but that was years ago. His office has so much paperwork that it would be impossible for me to look. The only person who could find anything in there would be the reverend himself. I don't know if he mailed them or still has the letters, but then again, he never throws anything away. I can ask him to look, but he might not do it for a while. The reverend is heading to California the day after tomorrow to attend his brother's funeral."

"I need those letters," Paul begged. "If I am there tomorrow, do you think the reverend would give me the letters, if he can find them?"

"Maybe."

"Ok, I'll be there!"

After hanging up the phone, every emotion about Nell that Paul desperately tried to bury over the years all began to unravel. The tears continued to fall heavy, making Paul wail. *She wrote back! She did want to be in my life and still loved me. I have a young daughter, and she is with the woman I love.* Not wanting to waste more time, Paul cancelled his date with Cindy, ultimately breaking up with her. He rushed to his bedroom and began packing his bags. He needed to find his missing loved ones and trace back any steps he might have missed through the years, hoping it was not too late. When he finished packing, Paul hurried into his car. Driving as erratic as Henry used to, he sped down the street.

Chapter 27

Hours later, Paul arrived in Rose, South Carolina. It was in the evening hours, and he rented a hotel room. Pacing in the room back and forth, Paul constantly watched the clock, wishing it was closer to the next morning. Why was he just now finding all of this out? He couldn't believe it.

I'm here, Paul thought. *No matter how long it takes, I'm going to get the answers as to where Nell and my daughter are.*

Paul could barely sleep in his bed, tossing and turning, eager for daylight. The late-night shows on television brought him no comfort to his anxieties. With hours still to go, Paul couldn't take it any longer, he showered, got dressed and left the hotel to find the Baptist Church that was mentioned in the letter. His body heavy, Paul broke into tears realizing how close the church was to the island where he once trained. He struck his fists against his car's steering wheel.

She was so close, Paul thought with wet, dull eyes. *Babe, I'm so sorry that I didn't know!*

Getting out of the vehicle, Paul rushed to the church doors, his vision blurred, and eyes reddened. The doors were locked, unnerving him. Paul sunk down to the concrete ground, tucking his legs in. He lowered his head and wrapped his arms around them. Buried images of the past began to flood his mind of him spending wonderful times with Nell in his old red vehicle, them dancing in their secret spots around Wood Oak High School, and their shared affections. Paul shook his head, thinking about all the lost time of him not being there to share the birth of his daughter and wanting to share moments with the girl that he loved. So much time had passed by that he couldn't help but cry out several times, envisioning himself being replaced by someone else as Nell's lover and father to his child.

Drained and unable to fill his lungs completely, Paul's chest quivered where he remained until sunlight began to rise, starting a new day. His back aching, Paul pushed back his head against the doors, closing his eyes. To him, he deserved the pain. Any physical pain he got, it didn't match how terrible his emotional or mental anguish was.

Two hours later, Paul felt someone kick him on the side of his shoes. His eyes shot open, noticing a seven-year-old Negro boy standing near him along with a few other children of various ages, no older than ten.

"I told you, he wasn't dead," one of the kids stated, his voice high.

"What's that white man doing here?" another child asked the first.

Rising to his feet, Paul observed that the church's parking was filling with cars and a few adults were nearby, talking amongst each other. They eyed him questionably and whispering to each other about him.

"You kids get on away from that man," one of the women ordered the kids, who mostly began to scatter.

"Can I help you?" an elderly Negro man asked Paul who appeared to be in his seventies.

"I called the other day," Paul said, "about Nell Jefferson and her daughter. I don't know who I talked to, but Nell was here almost four years ago, and I need to find her."

"She aint in any trouble, is she?"

"No, never! I'm her child's father and I've been searching for them for the last few years!"

"Aint she the one who left to be with Benny?" a woman asked the elderly man. "You know, the good looking one who works at the construction company about ten blocks away from here?"

"Yep," another woman chimed in, "that's the one!"

Paul stared down at his feet, his mouth downturned. His stomach was knotted, and he let out a heavy sigh. He hated himself, wishing he tried harder to change things from years ago. Looking at the sky, with his tear-soaked face and reddened eyes, Paul's hands fell to his sides, unsure of what more he could do about the confirmation of his replacement. He was done with love and any ties to such a feeling.

She moved on, Paul thought, a pained expression on his face. *I'm too late and I don't blame her. I'm such a fool to have ever let her go.*

"No," the elderly man corrected the woman. "That was Dorene who was having problems with her husband. Nell was the young mother with the light-skinned baby. She left a long time ago. Nobody knows for certain where some of these young mothers go after they leave. Most go back to their families or group homes for young, single, mothers."

"Nell left letters," Paul added, remembering the conversation from his phone call the day before. "May I have them, if they are addressed to me? Someone told me that a lady didn't mail them out, so since I'm here, I'd like to read what they say."

"I suppose," the elderly man replied. "You can come inside and wait while I go into my office and look."

Entering the building with the church patrons, Paul waited in a seating area. His eyes studied the facility, looking at the items within.

I'm not one who is religious and all, Paul prayed, *but I'll do anything to have my girls back in my life. I know I've screwed up so many times with women, but, please, just give me a moment, even if it's a second, to see Nell and our daughter. Nell, if you're out there, I still love and miss you. As hard as the reality is of you being taken in the arms of another man, I still want you in my life. I want to be a good father to our daughter, and I'll go anywhere to be near. Give me a second chance!*

"Here you are," the elderly man said, giving Paul two unopened letters that had stamps on them, unmarked by the post office, addressed to him.

"Thank you," Paul said, taking the letters. He opened one and began to read it.

Paul,

I hope that recruit training is going well for you. I waited to hear back from you but never got an answer. I had the baby a few weeks earlier than anticipated and had to go to the hospital. They asked me if I wanted to put our daughter up for adoption and I said no. I know that some people might disagree with my decision, but she is all that I have left, besides you. Sending her to be with someone else would be something that would have been too much for me to handle. When I hold and see her, I think of how beautiful our relationship was against all odds. I want her to grow up knowing how special you are to me and hope that one day, she can have someone

treat her with as much love and care as you treated me. I know it's going to be hard raising a baby at our age, but sometimes I just think, when has life ever been easy for anyone? We all have hardships, but this is one that I am willing to take on, knowing that in the end, it was out of love.

Love always,

Nell and Sharon

"Sharon," Paul uttered, opening the second letter.

Paul,

I've been in and out of the hospital with our daughter, Sharon. She's been sick for the past few days, and I've been staying with her as much as I can. While there, I ran into a guy who was related to a man named Justin Tillman, a guy who was in recruit training with you. I found out that your group had already left South Carolina. However, he told me that you had a relative during the graduation ceremony named Simon Dupont, who could help me locate you. I tried contacting him through the operator, but to no avail. I even had one of the church members drive me to the address listed for him, but nobody would let us through the gates. We begged to see your uncle, but not a single person would

listen to us nor let us through. The police were called, and we were ordered to not return to the property.

I truly do not know what else to do to communicate with you. I have no other address other than your old place in Magnolia at the garage. I will start writing to you there since the people in Magnolia are nicer and are more likely to give my letters to you.

Love always,

Nell and Sharon

With manic energy, Paul rushed from the church, driving until he reached a payphone. He shoved the coins into the slot, asking for the operator to connect him to Holiday's Garage in Magnolia, Louisiana. The phone rang until there was a click.

"Holiday's Garage," Luke's familiar voice answered.

"Luke," Paul said, his voice hurried, "it's Paul!"

"Paul," Luke cried out, his voice jovial, "how you been? It's been a while since I've heard from you!"

"Fine," Paul answered. "Luke, is Mr. Holiday in?"

"No, he's retired and has been traveling," Luke replied. "His business is still open, but Aaron oversees operations. Oh yeah, since I got you on the phone, every month, someone's been sending letters addressed to you at the shop. We didn't have your current number or address to tell you about the letters, but we've kept them for you in a box. If you give me an address, I'll mail them tomorrow."

"Tell me, whose been sending the letters."

"Nell and Sharon Jefferson are always written. Who are they?"

"That's my family," Paul cried out, a smile quickly stretching across his face. "What's the address from the last letter they sent?"

"Hold on, let me check," Luke said. The phone paused briefly. "Says 4396 Peach Lane, apartment 135, in Rose, South Carolina."

"Thanks," Paul said, ecstatic. He gave his current address and number to Luke before hanging up the phone.

They are still here, Paul said to himself, cheerful. *I need to find out where that is located.* He drove back to the Baptist Church, asking for directions to the address. The church reverend informed him that it was twenty blocks away, giving him directions. Excited, Paul could barely concentrate, asking the directions repeatedly to make sure he remembered the route perfectly.

Paul followed the routes given to him, ending the drive in a lower-class neighborhood that was well maintained. The two-story apartment complex was not too far from a nearby park with children playing on the playground, laughing joyfully. His chest quivering, Paul scanned the faces of the children and parents, none of them familiar. Paul parked his vehicle in the parking lot and got out of the car. He opened the front door to the building, moving to the side to avoid being run over by some mischievous youngsters who were chasing one another. Paul quickened his pace, ending his eager sprint to apartment 135. His head up and alert, Paul knocked on the door, and waited.

Chapter 28

The door opened, revealing an elderly Negro woman, surprising Paul. Right away he got dizzy, barely catching himself before falling over. *Did Nell move again? I don't think I can take more of this!*

"Who are you?" the elderly woman demanded.

"I--I'm Paul Boudreaux," Paul told her. "I'm looking for Nell and Sharon Jefferson."

"What's your business?"

"I'm Nell's boyfriend, or at least if she still wants me to be. I'm also Sharon's father. I'm here to see them."

The woman studied Paul, widening the door, and allowing him inside. The tiny apartment was scarcely furnished with a faded modest couch and sofa. There was a worn coffee table and carpet. The coffee table had stacks of paper that contained drawings and scribbles done by a young child. Nearby was a small assortment of animal toys sitting in random places such as near the couch pillow and by the single window.

"Don't you make too much noise," the woman warned him. "The baby is asleep in her room."

"May I see her?" Paul asked, trying to not appear too eager to make the woman mistrust him. The elder beckoned for Paul to follow her into one of the backrooms. Biting his lip, Paul got a fluttery feeling in his stomach upon entering the room and stepping closer the bed. Sleeping in the bed was an adorable youngster, months away from her fourth birthday, with olive toned skin and curly black hair dressed in a bright yellow gown. Her chest rose and fell as she slept soundly.

Warmth began to infuse Paul's body. He leaned closer to caress her soft cheek with his fingertips. All of his past tensions melted away.

"Hey baby," Paul whispered, his voice almost cracking. Closing his eyes as happy tears began to fall, Paul wanted to lift the child into his arms and never let her go but resisted the urge. He would have been a mere stranger, frightening her. Instead, he imagined himself doing so, eager to make it a reality soon. "Where is Nell?"

"She should be finishing her day job at the restaurant. Today is one of her short days. You must be as excited as I am for her completing her night classes to get her high school diploma last month."

"She did?"

"You didn't know? She's been doing that for a while, taking a class here and there at night and working during the day. I would know, I watch the baby while she is away; sometimes Gloria from down the hall watches her with her kids."

His face upturned; Paul wanted to shout for joy. *Babe, you did it after all! I'm so proud of you! I knew you'd find a way!* Suddenly, reality hit him, was there still a chance for *them*? Paul thought about the deal he made in his prayer about not caring if Nell were with someone else, full of sadness. *A deal is a deal.*

Hearing the front door to the apartment creek open and footsteps entering, Paul listened to the familiar sound of the voice he missed over the years calling out the name of the woman that was with him. The elderly woman, exited the child's room, heading back to the living room.

"Mrs. Alexander, I'm home," Nell's voice called out.

"There's a young man here wanting to see you," Paul heard the elder say.

"Really now? Who is it? Where is he?"

"I forgot his name already, but he is in the baby's room. He says he knows you."

Paul heard the door opening and shutting again. He stared at the door, uncertain what to do next. Would she be mad at him? Would she tell him how she'd never want to see him again? He certainly had no right to say anything. He was the one missing throughout the years. Almost forgetting to breathe, Paul's limbs began to shake and he became lightheaded. The light footsteps were approaching, and his eyes almost blurred making out the figure nearing the door. Then, his heart nearly jumped through his throat when he saw Nell. She was as beautiful as ever, with a slightly fuller figure, dressed in a beautiful dark purple dress and black shoes. Her magnetic brown eyes pulled him in.

Spotting Paul, Nell's eyes widened. She stopped in her tracks, bringing her hands up to her lips to cover them. Her eyes almost seemed to be just as pained as her full lips that trembled. Nell took a step back, her eyes filling with tears.

His bottom lip trembling, Paul stepped forward, widening his arms. He burst into tears before crying out, "My babe!"

Overcome with emotion, Paul thought, *regardless of if she takes me back or not, for this moment, she is still mine.* He squeezed her tightly, holding onto the love that was his. Nell wrapped her arms around Paul, sobbing. She was soft and comforted him, like a ton of weights being lifted off his shoulders. There was a sharp hardness between their chests. Squinting, Paul pulled back slightly, seeing the necklace that held his old school ring, bringing a brief smile upon his lips. He studied Nell's tear-soaked eyes, questioning what she wanted. As if reading Paul's thoughts, Nell grabbed Paul's shirt collar and yanked him closer to her, she planted a deep kiss upon his lips, shooting him with adrenaline. Their breathing growing increasingly faster and audible, Paul pressed Nell against the bedroom wall, with a loud *thump*. Wedging himself between her legs, Paul grabbed Nell's thighs, lifting them and wrapping Nell's legs around his waist. A muffled moan escaped Nell's lips, but she grabbed a handful of Paul's hair, pulling his head back, and stopping him from going further.

His eyes hurt again and bewildered, Paul frowned, lowering Nell back to the floor. Pressing a finger to her lips, Nell grabbed Paul's hand, leading him from the room. She took him down the hallway into another room that had a bed. Closing the door behind them, Nell mischievously shoved Paul into the bed before getting on top of him to resume their love making.

Chapter 29

His breathing labored, Paul swallowed hard, regaining control of his accelerating heart. He was tired, briefly closing his eyes. Next to him, wrapped in his arm, Nell lay, her breathing also labored. Smiling, Paul squeezed her soft arm, stunned that she was there with him.

"I never thought I'd see you again," Nell said. "After all this time, I thought you'd forgotten about me."

"Never," Paul said caressing her. "I'd never forget about you, ever."

"Why'd you never write back?" Nell asked, resentment in her tone. "Did you change your mind about being a father and being with me?"

"I didn't know where you were. I called and wrote to every place I could think of, and I was out of the country for two years. I thought you were still somewhere in Illinois because I never heard anything back! I got your letters *days* ago, honest! There was this envelope that must have been stamped a million times before I got it! Then the people at this church gave me letters that weren't mailed because some lady didn't mail them! I don't even have the ones from the garage yet, but the letters from the church guided me to the ones there! I've been looking for you for almost four years. Luke was the one who gave me your address and I had to go back to the church to ask them where your place was. Nell, I came all this way because I still love you."

Nell looked into Paul's eyes, her eyes softening, "I still love you too, Paul."

Elated, Paul gave Nell a hug while she wrapped a leg around him. Paul motioned for her to get on top of him. He beamed with her resting on his pelvis. He intertwined her fingers in his, bringing her hands to his lips to kiss them.

"Nell, I want us to be together again," Paul spoke, a serious tone in his voice. "No more separations. I know we've lost contact for a while and that you have your own life here with your own goals, but Nell, I need you and our daughter back in my life. I'll do anything you want, just keep me in your life."

"But what about your family and your own life?"

"I don't care about what they think or anything else. Babe, I still want to marry you, if you want to marry me."

"You're proposing while we are both naked in bed?" Nell laughed.

"You got that right," Paul chuckled. "And I'll keep asking every day until you tell me yes. You're not seeing someone else, are you?" His eyes grew stone cold at the notion of Nell being in a relationship with another guy.

Over my dead body if I'm being replaced by anyone! Paul had absolutely no qualms about pounding another guy into a pulp to win Nell back if he had to. His body tensed, scanning Nell's face for the slightest hesitancy of any sort of indication that he had any type of competition.

"I haven't had time to date," Nell admitted. "I've been busy working and going to school to build a better life for myself and Sharon. Sure, a few guys asked me out, but I didn't want to be caught up in anything and risk losing our apartment. I'm barely making enough to pay the bills and babysitter."

Nell glimpsed at the door frame, her eyes getting tearful. She pulled away, sitting on the bed's edge.

"The past few years have been hard, you know," Nell told him. "I met this other single mother named Elsie Gaines at the church who also wanted to keep her baby. We would help each other out, saving money here and there, watching each other's children, and all. We got this place together, with me and Sharon staying in one room and Elsie and her child staying in the other. Things were going well until she decided to go back to her abusive ex. With her gone, I took sole responsibility of the apartment, taking extra shifts at the seafood restaurant and having Mrs. Alexander watch Sharon for a few dollars. One day, a year ago, there was an article in the paper about my friend and her child being murdered by the child's father."

Paul moved next to her, draping an arm around Nell, "I'm sorry…That's horrible. Some people don't realize how important the lives of others are. I'm grateful that Elsie was there for you to help when I wasn't able to. I wish I could have met her; she sounds like an amazing friend… I don't want to imagine losing you and Sharon again. I was barely functioning as is."

"Yeah…"

"But, will you, Nell? Will you marry me? You still haven't answered."

"I don't know, Paul. It's been a long time…We aren't the same people we used to be, and I'm still hurt about so many things that happened between us. A marriage could only complicate things further."

"Tell me everything that hurt you and I will make it up to you."

"The whole living in separate places, not hearing from you for years, and you not being there during our daughter's birth. Those are the main things."

"I will live wherever you want me to live. I can't do much about the letters, but I will respond to every single one you sent once I receive them from Holiday's Garage. I'm sorry about Sharon, but I can be there for every birthday, holiday, or special event from this moment forward. I will drop everything."

"In reality, none of those things were your fault," Nell continued. "But, if you sincerely want to be in our lives, with marriage as a possibility, I'd like to see that we can be a *real* family living together and always being there for each other, then I can't say no."

Taking in a deep breath, savoring the moment, Paul let an extended exhale escape his lips, thinking.

"Sure, we can make that happen," Paul responded. "One question though… Nell, why weren't you living with your parents? I thought the whole point of sending you to Illinois was for you to be reunited with them."

"I got kicked out."

Paul squinted his eyes.

"*Kicked out*? Why would that happen? I thought they would be happy to see you again."

"My dad got upset because he thought my life was going nowhere as long as I was involved with you. He has this strong belief that I wouldn't finish school, remain an unwed mother, and because you're…"

"*White?* No surprise there… That's his problem. We certainly are beating the odds, aren't we? So, you don't talk to your family at all?"

"They moved into a better neighborhood, but I still communicate to my mother and siblings. My dad refuses to have anything to do with me, but enough about him… I just can't believe that you're here. What happened to you after you left recruit training?"

"I did my two years in the marine corps and I'm in the reserves right now. I'm taking some college classes as a double major in business and education. I started a year ago and have a few more to go."

"That means, you'll be leaving again," Nell said, her tone frustrated. She began to leave the bed, but Paul grabbed her hand, stopping her, with desperation in his eyes.

"I want you and Sharon to move in with me in Alabama or we can get a place here together," Paul suggested. "Like, I said, whatever you want to do. I can always go to another school."

"How is that going to work out for either of us? Moving takes time and money. Also, Sharon doesn't know you and would only be confused. Not to mention, if our relationship doesn't work out, I would be at risk for becoming homeless again with a small child."

"We could at least try. Since you are finished with school, at least come with me to Alabama. I'll pay for everything. It can be like a vacation, only an extended one to see if this is really what we both want. Sharon will get to know me, and we can reconnect, but will be living together. Would you be willing to do that?"

Biting down on her bottom lip, Nell contemplated Paul's offer, eventually agreeing.

Chapter 30

Later that day, after they both redressed, Nell introduced Paul to their daughter. Paul couldn't believe how much of a resemblance that Sharon had to her mother, only visibly having Paul's grey eyes. The little girl stared at Paul with her eyes shifting from one parent to the other at the lunch table.

"Paul is your daddy," Nell told the little girl. "We are going to go on a trip with him for a few days."

The more Nell talked, the more bewildered the little girl stared. She clutched onto her brown teddy bear and began to stick her thumb in her mouth. Right away, Nell gently pushed the girl's hand away, removing her thumb from her mouth. Whenever Sharon's eyes would fall upon Paul, there was a strong indication of mistrust that Paul refused to accept as a reality between him and his own daughter. He needed to build a form of trust and he needed to do it soon.

"So, who is that?" Paul asked Sharon, gazing at her toy bear.

Sharon gawked at Paul, not answering his question. She climbed from her chair and got closer to Nell, hiding near her.

"That's her bear, Bubba," Nell told Paul. "She carries him around wherever she goes. Sharon is shy around strangers, but once she knows you, you'll see that she acts more like you than me. I was supposed to take her with me to run a few errands, but maybe she can stay with you and you both can get to know one another. Would you be up for doing that? I'll be back in about four hours."

Absolutely," Paul said. "She isn't allergic to anything is she?"

"Nope, nothing. She usually likes to go outside in the park, but if she scrapes her knee or anything, there are bandages in bathroom cabinet above the sink."

Nell began collecting the lunch dishes, putting them into the sink. She began to wash them. Sharon stood near her mother, wrapping an arm around her mother's leg.

This is going to take some work, Paul realized. After the dishes were cleaned, Nell squatted down in front of the little girl.

"Mama's going to the store," Nell told her. "Daddy's going to stay with you, okay." Straightening back up, she attempted to bring the child closer to Paul, but Sharon refused, taking steps back, and whimpering. The closer Nell tried to get her to Paul, the more the little girl began to wail uncontrollably. Nell gave Paul a sympathetic look before turning back to Sharon. "You want to play with Bubba?"

Sharon nodded, gradually calming down.

"You want to show daddy Bubba's friend, Sprinkles?" Nell asked their daughter.

The girl nodded.

"Go and get him," Nell said.

Running into the living room, Sharon returned with a stuffed pink pony with white hair.

"Show daddy," Nell instructed the girl, nodding towards Paul.

Sharon stretched out her arm, giving Paul the toy. Grinning, Paul accepted it. Joyful, he made the pony seem as through it were also happy, giving it a cheerful bounce. The motion brought a smile to Sharon's face, doing the same with her toy bear.

"I'm going to take a quick bath," Nell told Paul. "Play with her for a bit and I'll be back." She walked into the bathroom, leaving them.

Unsure what more to do, Paul squatted down to the kitchen floor. He was still holding the toy horse in his hands. Sharon got on her knees. She began bouncing her bear up and down, mimicking it walking across the floor. Paul did the same but had his toy approach hers. Sharon shot him a curious glance, slightly moving nearer. Merrily, Paul began to hum a cheerful tune, making the toy horse move as if it were dancing. Sharon began to giggle, making her toy move as if it were dancing as well.

"You have more friends who want to dance?" Paul asked, using the same approach Nell had shown to include toys to help them bond.

"Yes," Sharon shouted in her adorable voice, pushing herself back onto her feet. She ran back into the living room, grabbing more stuffed animals one by one.

Paul rose from the floor, grabbing the first two stuffed animals. He walked into the living room and sat down on the carpet, watching his daughter gather more toys. Sharon dropped a few on the floor, rushing to rejoin Paul. Together, she and Paul gathered several toys, pretending to have a dance party.

Several minutes later, Nell reentered the living room refreshed from taking her bath, brushing her teeth, and having a change of clothes. She did a double take seeing how much fun Paul and Sharon were having on the floor, wishing that she had the time to join them. It was time to go, but she took a mental picture of that moment, not wanting to ever forget the joy that she was viewing between Paul and Sharon.

Days later, Paul and Nell put in the paperwork to have Paul's name added to Sharon's birth certificate, changing her last name to Boudreaux. Then, Nell and Sharon began to stay with Paul in his apartment, eventually moving into a bigger one that contained two bedrooms instead of one. Over the summer, Paul and Nell had a small wedding in Illinois with relatives and friends who chose to attend. Then, the new family moved into a three-bedroom house in Camellia, Alabama where Paul and Nell decided to continue working on their schooling.

Nell applied to several schools, but only got accepted into one college in Alabama near Paul's school, a Negro college that had a competitive program for nursing students. That meant that Nell would need to work harder than ever to get into the program after taking the required prerequisites. Paul financed his wife's education wanting her to focus on school without the added stress of working. Whenever they needed a babysitter, Paul hired a teenage neighbor named Ginger Reeves who came from a family that he knew was not prejudiced.

Paul continued to do well in his classes, always having a smile on his face, especially when he would return home to be with Nell and Sharon. Sharon was a very lively child who turned four years old, a week before Nell's twenty second birthday. Whenever Paul would come home, he would take Sharon into his arms, lifting her up to give her a big kiss on the cheek. He would tell her how much he loved her, never tiring of saying, "I love you" and being fond of hearing those same words returned to him from his daughter.

One evening, Paul was lounging on the couch viewing a children's program with Sharon. Sharon liked watching shows that had other children and animals. Whenever the show would have a sing-along, she loved singing to it, even when she would sometimes mix up the words. She would rest next to Paul, who would have his arm wrapped around her, joining in the songs. That is, unless Sharon leapt to the floor to do dance moves encouraged by the hosts of the shows. It was hilarious watching how thrilled the little girl would get to participate in the activities. Sharon was boisterous, full of energy, and love, a great contrast to how Paul had viewed her when they first met. His daughter quickly became a daddy's girl.

Standing next to Sharon, Paul chuckled as they marched to the rhythm instructed on Sharon's favorite children's show, Mr. McMagic. It was cute seeing her tiny legs and feet stomp down next to his. Then, they were instructed to shake their heads. Sharon shook her head, her curly black hair shaking wildly.

Riiinnnnggg! Riiiiinnnnnggggg! The telephone rang.

"Keep doing what you're doing," Paul directed his daughter, entering the kitchen beaming. Sharon laughed out loud, dancing to the instructions given on the show. Paul picked up the phone and pressed it against his ear, standing between the kitchen and the living room.

"Hello," Paul answered, his voice jubilant.

"Paul," his uncle, Simon's voice responded, "I reviewed the documents you submitted and approved of them."

"Thanks," Paul said. "That means a lot to me. I know you didn't necessarily agree to my marriage, but I am glad that you are helping me with all the legal documents. Uncle, I would still like for you to come over and spend some time with us and meet my wife and daughter."

"I most certainly do *not* agree with your marriage," his uncle agreed, "and wish to no longer have anything to do with any aspect of it. You would have been wiser to have kept that woman as merely a lover and give her a lumpsum payment to care for the child, without involving marriage. However, you are nearing the age in which you are to be more independent with your affairs. Let's hope you do not repeat the same mistakes you have done during your younger years."

"Basically, you're saying that I shouldn't have married anyone or have children."

"Correct. You've opened yourself to vulnerability. At the very least, for any marriage, it should have been to the same race *and* class."

"I can't speak on race, but they became the same class as I through marriage and birth. My father wasn't as wealthy as my mother, but they still had an excellent marriage. They didn't want me to go to one of those fancy schools to grow up thinking I was better than other people and I'm glad that they did what they did. I don't want to grow old and lonely, having more regrets."

"Then, we both shall see the result of your great investment in this 'family' of yours."

Chapter 31

"You've got to be kidding me," Paul gasped over the phone, that weekend. "You and *her*? How on earth did that happen?"

"It just did," Henry told him. "I went back to work at Holiday's Garage and ran into Molly a couple of times at the bowling alley. We argued a few times and hit it off."

"Wow, *you're* going *steady* with someone. Good for you! Welcome to the club!"

"It's only been a month, so I don't want to jinx it. How are things going there? When are you and the family coming back down for a visit?"

"Sometimes it's weird to hear *you* say that" Paul replied. "But, I'm glad that you do. I am lucky to be here with them at all. Since I was an only child, I wasn't supposed to go to Vietnam. They were supposed to have kept me in the states and had me stationed some place like North Carolina or California. Oh well, I served our country alongside lots of amazing people and have no regrets about that. Anyway, the family and I plan on heading down that way next summer. Nell and I will be taking time off from our classes to take a break and have a nice long vacation. I was thinking of getting a camper, that way we can see more of the east coast before heading towards Magnolia."

"Yeah, well, Nell wasn't too bad, and neither were several people I served with that are like her, if you catch my drift. Last thing anyone cares about is skin color while serving… For a twenty-two-year-old, you sure are taking fatherhood seriously."

"I sure am. My parents always went on long vacations each summer in June, and I plan on keeping the tradition alive with mine. Remember when it was July and my folks would have friends from out of town stay at the family cabin so that everyone was all in one place to socialize, spend time outdoors, and go into town. It's a shame what it's become now, having to be boarded up."

"Yeah, it was really nice inside," Henry agreed. "I remember that green couch that everyone used to fight over. It was so nice and comfortable; better than any bed I've ever slept on! Remember when the adults would be in the living room and we would sneak inside some of the rooms, hide under the beds or in the closets and pretend to be ghosts?"

"That was fun," Paul said snickering. "Mrs. Hilbert was a good sport about it. She talked back, knowing it was us and played along."

"Unlike Alvin who cried like a baby to his dad."

"He was six!"

"So…"

"So, he's going to be scared!" Paul laughed.

Nell entered the kitchen carrying two big paper bags full of groceries. She gave him a wink before placing the bags onto the kitchen counter.

"I got to go," Paul said to his friend. "The wife's here and I have to help put away the groceries. I'll call you later."

"Later, pal."

Paul hung up the phone. He began taking a few food items from the grocery bag.

"You could have stayed on the phone," Nell said. "It's just these two bags." She began pulling out a few cabbages. Paul began putting the items into the refrigerator.

"Sharon is napping in her room," Paul informed Nell. "You can sit back and relax. I have everything covered."

"I have to get dinner started."

"I had some takeout delivered and it's on the other side of the counter."

"Really? What did you get?"

"Shrimp alfredo pasta from the seafood restaurant down the street."

"You're so sweet, thank you," Nell said, closing the refrigerator door. Paul wrapped his arms around her from behind, nuzzling against her. He could smell her alluring perfume, heightening his senses. He kissed the nape of Nell's neck.

"But," Paul whispered in her ear, "I'd rather have my dessert early and I'm certain that you will taste just as good as you smell."

"You're such a Casanova, Paul," Nell giggled, raising her hand to pull him closer. "I need to be careful when I am around you!"

"Too late," Paul flirted. "I've already captured you and you already know what happens each time I do." He continued to neck while using his hands to unbutton Nell's shirt from behind. When the last button was undone, Paul lowered her shirt, exposing Nell's back. Paul tugged at his own shirt, pulling it above his head to remove it. While he was doing so, Nell turned grasping his belt buckle. Paul dropped his shirt to the floor, ready to have an exhilarating encounter with Nell before she took the tip of her finger and lightly trailing it horizontally against his skin between his lower stomach and groin. The touch was so sensitive and tingly it caused Paul let out a screech, stumble back, coiling away from her.

"Nell, what the heck," he cried out, his face grimacing.

Nell began to laugh.

"What you do that for?" Paul demanded. "You know I'm ticklish in that area!"

"If you want to capture someone, you shouldn't be sensitive in so many areas," Nell told him winking.

Chapter 32

Nell

Turning to the side, Nell stared at Paul's sleeping face. He was snoring softly, and his chest slowly raised and lowered between breaths. It shocked Nell each time she thought about it, to have someone as considerate as Paul be her husband who loved her unconditionally. He had always wanted the best for her ever since they got together. She was surprised to see that he still carried the old handkerchief she had given him years ago and loved that she still carried his school ring. Their marriage bands were just as special. Inside the wedding bands were a simple word, "Always."

"Why that word?" Nell asked Paul months ago.

"It sums up my love and devotion to you as your husband," Paul said. "There is no limit, no ending. It's a simple word that means a lot."

"I love you too, Paul," Nell whispered, feeling blessed. She rose from the bed and entered the bathroom, taking a long bubble bath. Afterwards, she brushed her teeth and dressed for the day. It was the weekend and she needed to go to the library to study with a few classmates from her biology class, but first, she had to take care of her loved ones. Nell removed the eggs, bacon, and cheese from the refrigerator and began preparing breakfast. She also put some toast in the oven.

Paul likes his scrambled eggs a little runny, Nell thought adding more milk to the eggs before putting them in the skillet. The appetizing aroma of the breakfast items began to fill the kitchen, making her mouth water. After everything had been prepared, she began setting the table.

"Good morning," Paul's voice said from the entrance of the door. He gave her an affectionate smooch. "I'm taking Sharon out with me to run a few errands. Then, when you get back home from your study group, I'll go and work on my assignments." He left the kitchen to walk into their daughter's room, leaving Nell to finish setting up the table.

Moments later, Paul returned with Sharon hand in hand. Sharon yawned, rubbing her eyes with her hand. Her eyes widened.

"Daddy, we forgot Bubba," she told Paul.

"Uh oh, hurry and get him before he misses breakfast," Paul told her, watching the youngster rush back to her room.

"You are a lifesaver," Nell told Paul, placing the food on the table.

"And so are you," Paul said giving her a thumbs up.

Sharon reentered the kitchen, holding Bubba. She placed him in his usual "seat" next to her plate on the table. Picking up her piece of buttered toast, Sharon took a bite from it. Then, she pressed the toast near Bubba, pretending that the bear was eating as well.

"Next summer, would you like to head back to Magnolia for a visit?" Paul asked Nell. "I was going to take Sharon with me to check out a few campers and go to the zoo afterwards."

"Sure," Nell said, "that sounds like a great idea! Are you sure you'll be fine with watching Sharon while I'm gone? I know you have a lot on your plate with all the classes you're taking."

"It's perfectly fine. I always study ahead of the class and it's no big deal. Enjoy your study session. I'll take over from here. Just leave your plate in the sink and I'll wash it. I love you."

"I love you too, thanks," Nell said, giving Paul a quick smooch. She finished her meal, put the dish in the sink, grabbed her purse, schoolbooks, a notebook, a pencil, and walked outside the family home. She got into the red vehicle Paul had given her months ago and began her drive to the library.

Nell thought at her old friend, Elsie. They both had a lot in common, including their shared desire to become nurses. It was unfair that she lost her life before making that dream a reality. Nell gazed at the sky.

Once I become a nurse, she promised, *not only will I walk across that stage for me and my family, but for Elsie and her son as well. Elsie, thank you for being such an amazing friend during one of my most difficult times.*

The streets weren't crowded that early in the morning. That was usually the case for the weekdays when parents would be dropping off their children or driving to work. Nell stopped in front of a red light and waited for the light to change. When it did, Nell pressed the accelerator, only to slam on the breaks when another vehicle flew by in front of her, coming from the left of her. Luckily, she avoided the accident. Her heart racing, Nell took a deep breath before resuming her drive. Suddenly, another car began blaring its horn at her, swerving to the left of the vehicle.

"What on earth," Nell shouted, veering the car to the side to avoid getting sideswiped. The offending vehicle swerved in front of hers, barely avoiding getting hit. Stunned, Nell, hit the breaks again. The vehicle behind her slammed on its breaks, blowing its horn. The first vehicle took off, leaving Nell wondering what had just happened. Her blood pressure began to elevate as she straightened the car, pulling it to the side of the road. Parking the car, Nell tossed her head back looking at the car ceiling.

Tap! Tap! Tap!

Nell turned to the front passenger window, seeing a blonde-haired woman in her early twenties tapping on it.

"Are you okay?" the woman asked. "You almost got into a pretty bad wreck!"

"I'm fine," Nell said, suddenly feeling nauseous. She threw open the car door, vomiting outside. Grabbing her sides, she keeled over, moaning.

The blonde woman rushed to the driver's door, pressing her hand against Nell's back, and pushing her hair back with her other hand.

The woman had on an off-white apron that had splotches of acrylic paint on it that covered her pink shirt and yellow pants.

"Ma'am," the woman said, "Why don't you come inside the art studio? I can get you a glass of water!"

Nell nodded, climbing out the vehicle, shutting the door, and following the woman inside the art studio. The art studio had a big room where different people were in the middle of working on their paintings. One woman had a bucket of paint in one hand that had a ruler sticking from it. Before her was a canvas that already had bit of paint on it. The woman grabbed the ruler, taking it from the bucket of paint, hurling its contents onto the canvas. Nearby was another painter who was gazing down at the picture of a flower, painting a copy of it onto her canvas.

"Wait here and I'll get you some water," the blonde woman told Nell, guiding her near a chair and going into another room. Nell sat down, still queasy.

The woman returned with the glass of water, handing it to Nell, who guzzled it down.

"Welcome to the Camellia Art Studio," the woman said cheerfully. "I'm Cindy Spearman and I work here part-time, teaching a few of the beginning art classes. What's your name?"

"Nell Boudreaux," Nell said, after pulling the cup away from her lips.

"*Boudreaux*?" Cindy repeated, her mouth falling open. "Not too many people around here carry that surname. This may sound farfetched, but would you happen to know *Paul Boudreaux*?"

"Yes, he's my husband."

Her eyes widening, Cindy swayed slightly, almost stumbling. She pressed her hand against her breastbone.

"*Husband*?" Cindy gasped, giving Nell a sullen look, and pressing her lips flat, speechless.

"Why?" Nell asked, suspiciously. "How do *you* know Paul?"

"We're old friends," Cindy said, giving an overly enthusiastic pitch to her voice. "I haven't seen him in a while. You should tell him to stop by sometime at the studio so we can catch up on old times. In fact, we are having an art show tomorrow evening. I'd love to see you both there, if you can make it."

"Sure," Nell replied, handing Cindy the empty glass back. "We are always looking for things to do on weekends. We'll be there."

Chapter 33

"So, where are we going for date night?" Paul questioned Nell, getting into the car the following evening.

"I'll let you know once we get there," Nell said, giving him the directions to the art studio. Over and over in her mind she wondered about Paul's relationship with Cindy. He never mentioned the woman before, but Cindy made it known that she knew him. *Maybe it's nothing and I'm being paranoid. She did say that they were friends.*

Paul's mouth grew drier, noticing the familiar route. His eyes began shifting off to the nearby streets when Nell asked him to park in the parking lot of the studio. The lot was almost filled with vehicles. Paul let out a muffled sigh, pressing the tips of his fingers against his forehead, after parking the car.

"Babe," he said, "are you sure you want to go *here?*"

"Sure," Nell told him, getting out of the car. She closed the door, rushing to the driver's side where Paul's facial expression was getting less cheerful by the minute. "I met this lady who told me that she knew you. She said that y'all were old friends and to bring you to the show."

Grabbing Paul's hand, Nell walked him into the studio that had a sign indicating that part of the art show would be in the back of the building. In the back, there was a medium sized crowd of artists and patrons with soft music playing in the background. There were chairs, tables that had refreshments, lights, etc. Near the building, there was an open door where people were coming and going into what seemed to be a gallery in the art studio. People of various backgrounds were laughing and talking amongst each other, hanging out outside or going inside to view more artwork which also consisted of ceramic sculptures, prints, etc.

Nell scanned the outside crowd, seeing the woman from earlier, chatting with a small crowd of people. *If they were only friends, then nothing should happen*, Nell thought. She drew Paul closer and tapped Cindy on the shoulder.

"Hey!" Cindy exclaimed, her eyes widening at the mere sight of Nell and Paul.

"We made it," Nell said overly optimistic. "Everything looks so beautiful! Thanks for inviting us!"

"I am so glad that you both came," Cindy told them. "It's been a while since I've seen you, Paul. We should really catch up on a lot of things. I have so much to tell you!"

"Certainly," Paul said, forcing a smile. He began to clear his throat. Turning to Nell, he leaned near her ear. "Babe, could you get me something to drink? My throat seems to be dry."

"S-sure," Nell said, squinting her eyes, curious as to why Paul was so eager to get rid of her. She pushed her way through the crowd, turning back around every so often. Nell watched as Paul began talking to Cindy and how the two began to leave, entering the building together.

Why are they leaving together, Nell wondered, stopping herself short of the refreshment table? *Has Paul lost his mind? After all his talk about wanting to be with me! He is leaving me, his wife, outside, and leaving with his "friend" to go inside! I guess I was right about people changing and from what it seems, not for the better when it comes to him!*

Nell's stomach dropped. Irate, Nell angrily snatched a cup from the refreshment table and began filling it with punch. Careful not to spill its contents onto herself, Nell pushed past the crowd, entering the art studio just in time to see Paul and Cindy enter a room she hadn't noticed before. Nell's eyes widened. She felt her hand get cold and wet, remembering that she was carrying the punch in a cup that was starting to bend from her increasingly tight grip. Loosening her hand, Nell's eyes began to tear, thinking about what a fool she was to bring her husband there that night to reconnect with a woman he was willing to ditch her for. Never in her life did Nell expect for Paul to have the urge to cheat. Nell's head grew light at the very thought of Paul making love to another woman. She knew Paul enjoyed flirting, making out, and having sex with her, but what if he wanted more, with somebody else? Maybe he was tired of just being with one person and had an itch that she couldn't scratch.

Woozy, Nell placed the cup onto the floor, unable to decide if she should just go home alone. *If it were nothing, why would they be going off into a separate room together and not just stay at the party?* Nell wiped a fallen teardrop from her face, choking back a sob. She lingered at the door that was cracked open, waiting to hear an erotic moment.

"How long have you two been together?" Cindy's voice was heard.

"Since we were both seventeen," Paul voice answered. "We were high school sweethearts and lost contact. It was no fault of either of us, but she's the reason why I couldn't take other relationships further. I love her and always will."

Nell peered through the cracked door. Paul and Cindy were still fully dressed, sitting in chairs across from each other in a room filled with unfinished paintings that rested on various easel stands.

"Is she the reason why that handkerchief is so special to you?" Cindy asked.

"Yes, it's one of the first things she's ever given me. She put her heart and soul into making it, even for someone like me who was an ideal jerk to her at the time. I didn't deserve someone as special as Nell, but she forgave me and opened herself up to the possibilities of being with me. We've been through a lot and have a beautiful daughter together despite all odds against us. I wouldn't trade them for anyone or anything in the world."

"I see," said Cindy. "I'm glad that you are happy, Paul. I still love you and wish you both the best. I appreciate you coming here tonight to support the arts."

"Thanks Cindy. Again, I apologize for hurting you back then. I was angry and frustrated, but that gave me no right to take it out on other people. You're talented and kindhearted. You deserve to be with the right person that will love you back."

"Thanks Paul."

"I better head back outside. I don't want Nell to worry."

Nell rushed back into the backyard, bumping into a few people along the way. She said her apologies, hurrying back to the refreshment table. When she spotted the punch bowl, she cringed, realizing that she had forgotten her cup on the floor. Grabbing an empty cup, she began filling it with punch. Nell turned around to view the backdoor of the building, but she did not see Paul reemerge.

Waiting, Nell questioned what was taking so long. Growing thirsty herself, she drank the punch from the cup before refilling it. Ten minutes went by before the door opened. Limping out, Paul was being helped by Cindy into the backyard. Dropping the cup, Nell rushed to Paul and Cindy.

"What happened?' Nell asked.

"I had an accident," Paul stated, scowling. "I knocked over a cup of punch that was on the floor, slipped, and fell. Why would someone leave punch *there*?"

Nell grabbed ahold of Paul, helping him to an unoccupied chair. She went back to the refreshment table, grabbed another cup of punch, and handed it to him. Upset and in agony, Paul shut his eyes drinking the cup's contents, not moving from the seat for the remainder of the art show.

When the show had ended, Nell drove them home and aided Paul into the house. Luckily, Sharon had already been put to bed by the babysitter. Nell assisted Paul to the bedroom where he collapsed into the bed. Cindy had already wrapped his ankle with a bandage earlier. Nell gathered a pillow and rested Paul's foot on top. Paul didn't bother to change out his clothes; he raised an arm above his head and closed his eyes. Nell noticed that a bruise was beginning to form on Paul's arm, the additional result of his bad fall. Guilt-stricken, Nell sat down next to Paul with her chin dropped to her chest and her posture slumped.

"I'm sorry about your ankle," Nell spoke, imagining how terrible the fall must have been and hating herself.

"It's no big deal, it's not like it's your fault," Paul stated. "Who would be dumb enough to leave a cup of punch on the floor? *The floor of all places!* Ugh! My whole right-side hurts, but my ankle hurts worse of all!" He cringed letting out a subdued wail.

"It's all my fault," Nell confessed, her voice cracking. "I'm sorry, Paul! I saw you leaving with Cindy and got jealous. I was listening to what y'all said to each other and accidentally left the cup behind. I didn't mean to hurt you, really, I didn't! Sometimes, I get insecure because of the time we were separated, thinking you might leave me to be with someone else."

"Nell, if you want to know the painful truths about what happened after we lost contact, I will admit that there were other girls and Cindy was one of them, but that wasn't until years later after not hearing from you, thinking you didn't want to be with me. Even then, I wasn't the same person I was when we were together. As much as I attempted to move on, the more bitter I became regardless of who came after you. There were many times when I couldn't even physically get intimate with someone else, no matter how much my body craved it! I simply couldn't do it. I never expected to hear or see you again, but when I did, I wanted to be whatever you wanted me to be as long as I could have you in my life again. Does that sound like I have the urge to cheat on you, knowing that I don't want to lose you?"

"I didn't date anyone," Nell confessed. "My dad made me feel horrible about dating and made it seem like I was his biggest failure. I had a few guys ask me out, but I said no, not wanting history to repeat itself. My dad would say that I would be replaced if another woman was ever in the picture and that didn't help matters much…I still thought about your letter from when you were in recruit training, asking to still be my boyfriend. When it came to those other guys, I'd never leave home for any of them, but for you, I would."

"Nell, you are not a failure and have done so many things that would have been impossible for many. Being a young mother was hard work and you managed to do a beautiful job raising Sharon. Then, while doing so, you found a way to go to night school to get your diploma, get a job, and find a place to stay. Nell, I understand that you value your father's approval to be a success in his eyes, but know that in my book, you are a success. I don't want to be the cause of you and your father having a family rift, but you say that you still talk and write to everyone else. Maybe, you could call or write to him as well highlighting your achievements. If not for him, but for yourself and at least, opening lines of communication."

"And what if he doesn't care to speak or write back?"

"At least you made the effort. It's not just for him, but for you. No matter what happens, I'm gosh darn proud of you."

"Paul…"

"Yes, babe?"

"How could you have problems down there? We have sex all the time and you're as hard as a rock."

"Nell, have you looked in the mirror? You're as foxy as all get out!" Paul chuckled, beckoning her to lay closer to him. Nell rested her head on Paul's chest, and he wrapped his arm around her. "Aaaannnddd…I love you, always remember that."

"I love you too, Paul."

Chapter 34

Monday evening, Nell pressed the phone against her ear, hearing it ring. She contemplated who would pick up the phone. Usually, it had been her mother who would have answered during the rare occasions that Nell would call, but this time, it was different.

"Hello?" the masculine voice answered.

"Dad," Nell spoke, "It's me, Nell."

"Yeah."

"I don't know if mom told you this, but I was able to go to night school and received my high school diploma, in South Carolina. Right now, I am taking classes to become a registered nurse at South Aster College in Alabama... I had the baby and named her Sharon. Also, even though you didn't attend the wedding, I am still married to Paul, and he's been an excellent father and husband..."

"Okay, good for you."

Nell paused, waiting to hear if her father would say more to her. She wanted to ask him if he were proud of her regarding anything she just said, no matter how small or what it was, but couldn't find the courage. Nell brought a finger up to her lips, biting the nail. She removed it when her stomach began to be fluttery again. Unable to cope with the silence much further, she hung up the phone, bursting into tears. She slumped down onto the floor, wiping her wet face with her hands.

In the next room, she peered at Paul who was asleep on the couch where Sharon lay next to him with Paul's arm wrapped around her. Shifting her position, the little girl wrapped her arm around her father, snuggling with a smile upon her sleepy face. Pulling herself together, Nell rose from the floor, straightening her position. She walked into the hallway closet, grabbing a brown blanket. She went into the living room, draping the blanket over the sleeping father and daughter.

Chapter 35

Tuesday evening, Nell sat in the library with some of her classmates from her algebra class. They were struggling, with a class average of a D between all five of them. Darrius Sikes, a twenty-eight-year-old Negro man who worked part time as a waiter had a pile of math books near him, scanning through each one in search for a simpler formula than the one given in class. Fortunately for him, he had the second highest grade out of everyone with a C. Nell's grade was the highest C, but the other three students had Fs.

"It's gonna be another long night," Darrius complained. "Any of you understand the problem yet."

"You told us, but I still don't get it," one of the women told him. She pointed to one of the math problems, asking Darrius several questions.

"Darn it, Olivia, now you got me all confused," Darrius grumbled.

"What you expect, that's why I asked," Olivia replied.

"We should go to Professor Howard's office," a man named Bruce Thomas suggested. "He's the best in the math department and can make anything look easy."

"That's why his class filled up first," Nell agreed. "I wish we knew before signing up for Professor Owens' class."

"Everyone who failed Professor Owens' class last semester hurried and signed up for Howard's this semester," Olivia Edwards added. "As soon as registration opened, Howard's class was filled within minutes. I tried going to Howard's office, but his office hours are always when I have another class."

"Why are all of you complaining when we should be studying?" a woman named Sandra Batiste noted. "The test is tomorrow, and we don't have time for all this foolishness. If we don't pass it, we might as well drop the class and retake it.

"Technically, I *am* passing the class," Darrius reminded her, tilting his head to the side and nodding.

"You should be, you been in school long enough to teach it," Sandra told him.

"As usual, you don't know what you're talking about," Darrius snapped back. "I've been working most of my life and starting my college career, just like everyone else at the table. Keep mouthing off disrespecting people and you will find yourself doing just what you're accusing me of."

"The library closes in thirty minutes," Bruce informed the table of students. "We need to get back on track."

Stuck on the math problem, the group decided to move onto the next formula, still lost, getting nowhere. Bruce tossed his pencil onto the table, slamming his book closed. He began gathering the books he took from the shelves, giving them back to the librarian at the counter, and returning to the group table to push his chair back in.

"Where you going?" Darrius questioned him.

"Home," Bruce indicated. "I'm not going to pass the test, so why waste more time trying to study?"

Restless, Nell began to speak.

"We could try my husband," she suggested. "He was really good with math in high school, but he'd never make it to the library in time before closing. We'd have to go to my house if anyone is willing to go."

"I'm going," Sandra said without hesitation, slamming her book closed and gathering her papers.

"I'm tired, but I'm going too," Darrius agreed.

They all returned the library books and followed Nell to her home in their cars. Nell couldn't believe that everyone was heading to her house. She never had visitors from school before in her new home and it was nearing ten o'clock, meaning the rest of the household would have been in bed. She swore under her breath, remembering that she didn't have time to clean up hours before leaving to go study at the library. She began to think about how humiliated she was going to be once everyone saw all the scattered toys.

Nell and her classmates parked their vehicles, gathered their belongings, and headed to the entrance of the home. Nell unlocked the door, turning on the lights to the living room that was surprisingly clean. Nell lifted her head towards the ceiling, mouthing, "thank goodness."

"Wait here and I'll get my husband," Nell said to her classmates, who began sitting with their books and other writing materials in the living room.

Nell went into the bedroom, observing that the bed had no one in it. The bathroom lights were on, and the door was closed. Nell knocked on the door.

"Paul," she called out, "are you there?"

"Give me a minute," Paul's voice responded back. Nell sat down on the bed. Suddenly, the bathroom door flew open with Paul standing there with a white towel wrapped around his waist.

"Where have you been, *Mrs. Boudreaux*?" he flirted, grinning naughtily. "You've been a *bad* girl keeping me waiting." He sauntered to the bed, pressing his lips against Nell's, and climbing on top of her. His skin was still damp from his shower and the towel soon fell to his side, exposing him. Nell tried to speak, but each time she attempted, Paul would kiss her with another passionate kiss. Moaning and breathing heavily, Paul pressed his body against hers until, without warning, there was a shriek at the door.

Startled by the unexpected scream, Paul leapt back, falling off the bed, and onto the floor. He turned to the bedroom's doorway, seeing an unfamiliar Negro woman standing there with her eyes wide and mouth covered by her hands.

"What in the world?" Paul cried out. "*Who are you*?"

Stunned, Sandra rushed down the hallway.

Paul turned Nell's way, his face paled, bewildered, and furious. He rose from the floor, snatching the towel from off the bed and wrapping it around his waist.

"What's going on?" he questioned her. "Who is that and what is she doing here?"

"I'm sorry," Nell said. "She's a classmate and we needed your help with our math class. Our study group couldn't figure out some of the formulas for our test tomorrow and I didn't think that you would mind. The teacher threw in a bunch of new stuff the last fifteen minutes of class and said it could still be on the test."

"You could have called before one of your classmates saw me *naked*," Paul said, an edge in his voice. He opened the dresser, putting on some black shorts and a plain white t-shirt.

"I said I was sorry! I didn't think we would be doing anything tonight."

"Nell, we have sex *every night,* unless it's that time of the month for you! Wait a minute…It isn't that time already, is it?"

"Will you lower your voice," Nell told him, her tone getting irritated. "I don't need everyone knowing our business! Could you just go with me to the living room and help us, please!"

Nell and Paul walked into the living room where the other classmates gawked at Paul, apart from Sandra who was covering her face partially with her hand.

"*He's* your husband?" Darrius gasped, raising an eyebrow.

"Mmmmm," Olivia uttered, titling her head, and giving Darrius the side eye.

Bruce began to chuckle, not saying a word. He shook his head with his eyes wide, staring down at his book.

"Yes, he is," Nell said. "Everyone, this is my husband, Paul. Paul, this is Darrius, Olivia, Sandra, and Bruce. We need your help with some algebra problems. You think you can help?"

"I-I should," Paul spoke, evading looking at Sandra and sitting down in the only other available spot, next to her on the couch.

"I heard a scream," Olivia noted. "What was that all about?"

"Nothing," Sandra said swiftly, sliding her body further away from Paul as far as she could. Rubbing the back of his neck, Paul picked up one of the math books from the coffee table.

"What page are you on?" Paul asked, tugging at his shirt collar. He peeked at the clock, noticing that it was 10:30 pm. He gave Nell a gaze with his eyes that read as, "do you know what time it is?"

Nell gave him a "just do it" facial expression, forcing him to comply.

"167," Darrius said.

The group opened their books, commencing the study session that continued well into the night and ending at 12 am. The classmates thanked the Boudreauxs and drove away to their own homes. Nell sulked viewing Paul's now incensed face. Without a word, he left the living room, returning to the bedroom. Nell trailed behind, entering the bathroom to take a bath to give Paul some space and time to cool down. When she reemerged from her bath wrapped in a bath towel, Paul was still laying in the same position with a scowl plastered on his face.

"I'm sorry," Nell told him slipping into bed next to him. "You're right; I should have called first. It won't happen again and I'm sorry Sandra saw you naked. The test is in a few hours, so we had to study tonight."

"I have a test in a few hours too, you know," Paul reminded her. "I get it, Nell, but try to be a little more considerate of my time as well."

"I'm sorry, I didn't know you had another test coming up."

"I'm not upset about the upcoming test. I'm upset because that study session interfered with my time with you. I've been going to classes all day, helping to take care of Sharon when the babysitter leaves, cramming, cleaning, and waiting for you to come home. Most days, our mornings are short, and we are busy throughout the day. I don't want to be a husband who only spends time with his wife on the weekends, but one who wants to be with you as often as I can. Nell, it's okay what happened with your study session, minus that embarrassing moment. But, I want to be selfish and have nobody interfere with our time together."

"I understand, Paul," Nell said. "I promise that during our time together, it will only be about us."

Slowly, Paul's angry face dissipated. He scooted closer to Nell, kissing her gently. Nell looked at the clock. It was 12:30 a.m.

"Sorry for keeping you waiting, *Mr. Boudreaux*," she said. "I've been a bad girl." She touched Paul's face with the back of her hand, drawing it downward. A flash of excitement sparked in Paul's eyes.

"Good," he said smirking, giving Nell a deep and prolonged eye contact. "Because this bad boy loves his bad girl." Nell removed her towel, kissing Paul to begin their intimate time together.

Chapter 36

Wednesday morning, it was thirty minutes before the algebra test. Nell and several of her classmates were gathered in one of the empty classrooms reviewing the formulas.

"That sure was nice of you and your husband to help us study last night," Darrius stated to Nell. "Tell him thanks again for us the next time you see him."

"But I don't get it," Olivia said to Nell, shifting the mood of the room. "Why would you want to be with a white man for? He looks good and all, but I could never see myself being with one of them. My ancestors would roll over in their graves if I ever did that willingly."

Straight away, Nell shot her an intense, cold stare. She folded her arms against her chest. One of her hands dug into her skin, giving it a tight grip before she released it.

"I'm with him because I love him," Nell said flatly. "Are *you* seeing anybody?"

Bruce pinched his lips together, burying his face behind his book. He leaned his ear sightly towards the bickering women. He mouthed, "Oh, shit," with his lips. A few more classmates began to turn their heads towards the two women, paying attention to what might happen next.

"She's with a white man?" a woman whispered to her friend who was sitting next to her.

"Shhh, I'm trying to listen," her friend shushed her, using her hand to wave her friend away.

"No, but if I were, it wouldn't be with one of them," Olivia told Nell. "Why be with a white man when we got all these good-looking black men on our own campus? I knew something was off when we drove to the other side of town, in the white area. You aren't one of these self-hating blacks, are you? It's strange that you are with Paul, as strong as his southern accent is. You can hear the racism in his voice the longer he spoke! I bet by the end of the day, even to your husband, your just anoth---."

"Shut up," Nell bellowed, slamming her math book down on her desk and rising from her seat.

"Hey, hey," Darrius spoke, getting between the women, spreading his arms out to put more space between them. "Not need to fight! Olivia, you need to watch your mouth. What they do is their own business, not yours. Paul didn't have to stay up all night helping us, especially since you had the most questions. Be more grateful. Not all southern white men hate black folk, and we don't need people like you giving them more of a reason to hate us. Nell has every right to be with whomever she wants to be with and they both seem happy together."

Olivia smacked her lips, rolling her eyes.

"She better pass the test today because she'll never be welcomed into my house again," Nell said sneering at Olivia. "You could have left at any time, if you had a problem, but you stayed there long enough to waste my husband's time to teach your ignorant behind."

"I didn't plan on going back," Olivia responded. "I'd rather take the class over before going back to 'massa' for help."

"Enough," Darrius barked, his voice making everyone freeze momentarily. "In case y'all forgot, we got a test in ten minutes! Study and stop all this bickering!"

Both women shot more incensed glimpses towards one another before returning to their books to study. Soon, it was time to leave to go into the other classroom to take the test. Nell waited until everyone left the room. She needed additional time to cool off from her horrible encounter with Olivia, trying to resist the urge to fight the woman for having the audacity to say those cruel words. Instead, Nell prayed that the horrid woman would fail the test and possibly fall down that trick step along the stairway to the math building, embarrassing herself. Nell went to the other classroom, avoiding Olivia and sitting down in the front of the classroom.

After the test was distributed, the class fell silent. Ten minutes into the test, some students got no further than writing their names. Nell was able to solve at least five of the problems easily, but the rest of the test was problematic with her not recalling ever going over certain math formulas as indicated in class or their book.

Nearby, Bruce was scanning through his test, mouthing, "damn," as his eyes fell onto the same tricky equations that Nell was struggling with.

Sandra's hand shot up from the middle of the classroom; the teacher approached her desk.

"Professor Owens," she said, "I don't remember us ever going over these types of math problems in class." She pointed at her test paper.

"Do the best you can," Professor Owens told her, resuming his walk across the classroom.

Nell bit the side of her pencil, turning back to the front side of the test. She squinted her eyes, realizing that the test had Professor Howard's name on it instead of Professor Owens! They were given a test that was created by another teacher! Nell's mouth fell and her eyes broadened. Her eyes shifted to see if anybody else had noticed the error.

"Keep your eyes on your own paper," Professor Owens instructed, coercing Nell to put her eyes back onto her own test.

Remarkably, Olivia was the first person to turn in her paper. Nell pondered if the woman had given up. Olivia gathered her possessions, stomping out of the room, indicating that she most likely did not pass.

Serves her right, Nell thought. *But when I prayed for her to fail, I didn't mean for the entire class to fail too!*

Refocusing her attention to her own paper, Nell abruptly had the urge to gag. Her stomach was doing flip flops. She fought back until stomach acid began to climb up her throat. Then, incapable to hold back any longer, her mouth flew open, vomiting over her test paper and part of her clothes.

"Come on now," a nearby student hollered, scooting his desk away from Nell's.

A few students began to squirm away from Nell, several stuffing their noses within their shirts. Professor Owens' lip curled as he made his way towards his desk, picking up a few tissues from his tissue box and giving them to Nell.

"You there," the teacher said pointing to a student seated near the door. "Get a custodian."

"I'm sorry," Nell spoke, wiping her mouth with the tissue.

"It stinks in here," a woman complained, pinching her fingers over her nose.

"Why don't you go to the bathroom," Professor Owens told Nell, pointing towards the door. Mortified, Nell left the room.

Chapter 37

When she returned home, Nell held onto her stomach, resting in bed. Near the bed was a glass of water on the nightstand. She was allowed to retake her test the following day and the class had to change rooms to finish theirs. She didn't go to the rest of her classes and went to the doctor on campus who confirmed her symptoms.

Hearing the creaking sounds coming from the front door of the home, Nell turned her head towards the bedroom door. Soon, little feet rushed inside, followed by denser steps.

"Mommy," Sharon cried out, hoping into bed with Nell. All smiles, the child cuddled next to her.

Not wanting to project her ill mood onto her daughter, Nell forced a smile.

"Hey, baby," Nell said, giving her daughter a kiss on the forehead.

"Mommy, why you in bed?" Sharon asked, tilting her head to the side. "I make you better." She puckered her lips, kissing her mother on the cheek.

"Thank you, baby," Nell told her. "I feel better already."

Paul entered the bedroom. He sat across from Nell, making strong eye contact, that read, "What happened?"

Holding onto Nell's hand, Paul gave it a gentle squeeze before turning to their daughter.

"Sharon, why don't you get Sparkles," he said.

"Okay," the little girl answered, climbing out of bed, and running into her room to find the toy.

"What did the doctor say?" Paul asked Nell, leaning in.

"I'm not pregnant, but too stressed out," Nell confessed. "I was taking the test and there were a lot of things on it that we didn't study for. I noticed that the test wasn't even made by our teacher! Why would he do something like that? Sometimes, I think that people want me to fail. If I don't pass, my grade was going to drop from a high C to a high D. If I'm struggling this early, it'll only get worse. I'm such a loser!"

"Maybe you should take some time off from school," Paul suggested. "If it's starting to affect your health, a break would do you some good."

"That'll put me too far behind!"

"You are going to school fulltime and have been worrying about your classes, especially the algebra one."

"If I don't succeed. I'll just be what my dad has always thought of me, a failure. The bad grades will just confirm everything he's ever said that had been negative.

Even after getting married and finishing high school, he still acted like it was nothing to him."

"Stressing over one difficult test is not evidence that you're a failure. It just means that the class is challenging. I know your grades mean a lot to you. Since you're being given a second chance to retake the test, I can help you study. Give me a few minutes to talk to Ginger to see if she can babysit for an hour or two."

"Thanks, Paul," Nell said. "How are your classes? You said that you had a test today. How did it go?"

"Fine," he replied. "I know I passed. My father's side of the family taught me everything they knew about business math, strategies, and the like. I was taught certain skills early, so a few things are simpler for me."

Paul strolled outside of the room, leaving Nell. Sharon sprinted into the room with another toy, placing it next to Nell.

"Sharon," Paul called from another room, "We're going to go next door to Ginger's house!"

Nell gave her daughter a kiss before the little girl ran outside the room to join Paul. The front door to the house opened and closed. Her stomach calmed, Nell got out of the bed and walked into the living room where she had placed her college books earlier that day. She flipped her math book to the pages that had the unusual formulas that she saw on the test. She scanned the examples, completely lost. Scratching at her temple, she observed that the formulas were two chapters ahead of what her class had been taught by Professor Owens.

The door to the home opened and closed again. Paul sat down next to Nell on the couch, and she handed him the algebra math book.

"Let's see what we are working with," Paul said, scanning the pages, taking it all in with an animated face.

"I don't know what I'm going to do," Nell told him. "I don't know how I managed to get a C. If I don't pass this test, my passing grade is as good as gone."

"It's going to be fine," Paul assured her. "If you get confused, tell me. Let's start …"

For an hour, Paul and Nell discussed the different equations. Every so often, Paul would come up with new examples for Nell to solve, with him checking and reviewing the answers. Time flew by faster than Nell anticipated, and the neighbor returned with Sharon.

"Just keep studying what we went over," Paul called out to Nell, taking Sharon into the kitchen to get her a snack.

Nell glowered, still somewhat confused. She didn't want to take up more of Paul's time. He seemed to be busy, picking up the slack that she already was feeling guilty about. She prayed that all the time Paul spent with her wasn't in vain, not wanting to upset him over a wasted study session and a failing grade.

That Thursday afternoon, Nell went to the professor's office to complete her test. She prepared herself for anything. If she passed her test with at least a C, she would still be able to hold onto her C average in the class. It wasn't the best grade, but it meant that she wouldn't have to retake the class and would have been her only C in all her classes which had either As or Bs.

Professor Owens took out a folder and handed Nell the test that she had been dreading. Her stomach began to act up again, but this time, it was not as intense. Taking a deep breath, Nell took the test in her hand. It was a new one, with Professor Owens' name typed on it. Nell studied the different math problems. They did not have the overly complicated equations that she had been cramming for, but the simpler ones that were reviewed in the previous classes and earlier study sessions with her study group and Paul.

"After you left, I observed that the class was given the wrong test," Professor Owens admitted. "The department secretary accidentally gave me another teacher's test and he had mine. I had to toss Professor Howard's test and give everyone the correct one. You, too should have the correct test."

Nell closed her eyes quickly, saying a muffled prayer of thanks.

"We won't be reviewing the other formulas that you saw on the other test until next week," Professor Owens added. "You have twenty minutes to complete your test."

That means, Nell thought, *that I'm ahead!* She began beaming, writing her name on the test, and jotting down her answers.

Chapter 38

Paul

"Next," the postal worker called out from behind the counter.

Paul approached the counter with his handful of letters to send out: letters to his buddies in Magnolia and a letter to the Jefferson family. He knew that things were still strained between Nell and her father, but he aspired that the duo would reconcile their differences. Nell told him about the phone call between her and Mr. Jefferson from days ago. She was upset by the shortness of it all, but Paul saw it differently. He believed they were making progress. At least, they were on speaking terms, somewhat, making him proud of Nell. However, since Paul knew that he wasn't liked by Mr. Jefferson, he thought that he, too, should offer an olive branch to his father-in-law, if not for himself, but to help Nell's progress with her relationship with her father in his letter:

Mr. Jefferson,

I am sending you a picture of your granddaughter, Sharon. She is four years old and is one of the happiest and cutest angels imaginable. During the holidays, I would love for you to come out to meet her with the rest of the family. You are always welcomed to see her at any

time, and we have an extra room at the house that serves as a guest room.

Nell is doing well in school. She is passing all her classes with hopes to become a nurse one day to share her skills and wonderful heart with others. She told me that you two were close when she was growing up and the stories that I hear, reminds me of the close relationship that I have with my own daughter. I apologize for unintentionally coming between you two, but I wanted to share with you, how appreciative I am to be with Nell. She is a go-getter, wonderful mother, and loving wife, all thanks to you and Mrs. Jefferson. Thank you for raising my beautiful wife to be the lovely person that she is today. I am forever grateful to have her and our daughter in my life.

Paul

He handed the postal clerk the letters and returned to his vehicle. Inside, he reopened the box sent to him by Luke from Magnolia, Louisiana months ago. It contained all the letters Nell had sent him throughout their missing years together. Next to that box was another, addressed to Nell that he had been working on. As promised, he made sure to respond to each letter, to give to her later that day.

I can't speak for Mr. Jefferson, but I hope that he will at least consider calling or writing to Nell, Paul thought.

Starting the car, Paul drove off into the distance, following the route he once dreaded. It was the same gorgeous area with the mansion that was miles away from the main gate that seldom permitted access to visitors. Upon entry and after the long drive, Paul parked his vehicle. He was greeted by the mansion's servants and entered the building to the main study of the stern man who had his own blockages. Paul's uncle, Simon, stood near the tall window, gazing outside, with his back turned towards him, not uttering a word to acknowledge his presence. There was nothing more to say that hadn't already been discussed. The man had never been much for words and almost void of emotions, but still, Paul either called or visited him weekly whenever he had the chance. Paul wasn't sure if it were out of his own curiosity, but his uncle seemed to have so much, yet so little. His twin hadn't spoken to him in years, and Paul was his sole family member that visited.

Paul sat down in the chair, placing a hand beneath his chin, waiting in silence while the grandfather clock ticked away, creating the only sound within the room.

Thirty minutes later, Paul rose from his seat, placing his letter onto his uncle's desk and walking away, leaving the room.

His uncle, Simon sustained his gaze outside the window, ultimately watching Paul's vehicle leave the property.

"Get my car ready to take me to Wood Oak," Simon ordered the butler who stood near the doorway. He approached his desk, seeing the letter that remained. Sinking into his chair, Simon opened it.

Uncle Simon,

I know you are not one to celebrate such an occasion, but happy birthday to you. Thank you for all that you have done for me and my mother by visiting her grave often. It is apparent that you two were close. Uncle, you are always welcomed into my home with my wife and daughter. I would love to see you happy again. While I cannot bring my mother back, I'm sure she would want you to be around family. We are your family and are here, should you allow yourself to be open to the possibilities. In the meantime, I will continue to visit you from time to time.

Paul

Chapter 39

"Whatever happened to Simon's twin?" Henry asked over the phone.

"He got married and moved away to Texas," Paul informed him. "They don't talk, but it's mainly due to Uncle Simon's choosing. It's remarkable that he gives me the time of day. My mother and him used to talk every weekend over the phone. Sometimes, he and his brother would show up at the house, but after my parents died, he pretty much shut down."

"Can you imagine grieving that long? Hasn't it been like almost twelve years?"

"Yeah, but I get it. I miss my parents too."

"Stephen's been wanting to get in contact with you for a while. I wasn't sure what to tell him after all the drama that transpired in Wood Oak. I have his new phone number, if you want it. He wanted you to give him a call."

"Sure, why not."

After Henry gave Paul Stephen's number, the two resumed their conversation for an additional ten minutes before finishing. Then, Paul dialed Stephen's number. The phone rang three times before it was answered.

"Hello," the familiar voice on the other end of the phone line answered.

"Stephen, it's Paul," Paul stated.

There was a thrilled surge of laughter.

"*Paul*," Stephen's voice rang happily, "I can't believe it! I *finally* get to speak to you after all these years! The guys and I missed you, pal!"

"Really? I thought everyone hated my guts!"

"What? Never! The team and I were looking forward to a winning basketball season with you leading us but, you were gone! We didn't win *any* games after you left. We assumed you were sick and would be out for a few days but realized that you were gone after so long. People began to ask your cousin, Bill, what happened to you. Of course, he wouldn't tell us anything. He did, however, make a big deal that someone shot him in his hand during a hunting trip. He got into a few more arguments with a few of the guys. Several of us wanted to pound him so many times, but we didn't because of you and the fact that he was already injured. Before the Wilkerson's moved, they gave me their new address to keep in contact with Henry because I asked. Paul, when do you plan on coming back to Wood Oak? You, me, and the rest of the team should get together and hang out for old times' sake."

Paul wrinkled his nose. *Getting together with the guys?* As simple as that sounded, it would be out of the question for him. He remembered how terrible the high school had gotten when it got integrated with Nell, Martin, and the other Negro students. None of his friends wanted people like them at the school, which, unfortunately, included him at first. How could he even begin to think of what to do? Should he keep his family secret or have things out in the open?

I can't do this, Paul thought. *What kind of husband and father would that make me if I didn't care enough for my family to be brave enough to claim them? As much as I like my old friends from my old home, I love my family and will always put them first, even if that means losing some people along the way.*

"Stephen," Paul said, "Remember that girl named Nell Jefferson who came to our school in the fall of 1969?"

"Yeah," Stephen replied, "she was that colored girl who was always quiet and sat in the back of the classroom. What about her?"

"She's my wife."

There was brief silence before a burst of laughter from Stephen.

"Paul," his friend said, "do you realize what you're saying? You must be losing your mind telling crazy stories like that!"

"It's true" Paul told him. "We're married and we have a child together."

"*What*?" Stephen's voice deepened. "You're kidding me!"

Paul could already imagine the stunned look upon his friend's face. He didn't care anymore about what others thought. He hadn't spoken to his old Wood Oak friends, except for Henry, in the last few years anyway. If Stephen had a problem with whom Paul wanted to be with, that would be his own problem.

"Why, Paul?" Stephen asked. "*How?* Was Nell the reason why you broke up with Nancy? Did Nancy know before she started dating Bill?"

"Yes and no," Paul confessed, "Yes, I broke up with Nancy to be with Nell. No, Nancy didn't know about Nell. I didn't want to tell anyone because of how things were in Wood Oak. It just happened."

"I don't know what to say," Stephen admitted after a prolonged pause. "A lot of things happened back then. I don't blame you for being silent, especially knowing how your relatives and everyone at the school were."

Paul scratched his cheek. He was glad that he was sitting down in the kitchen. The conversation was something that he had wanted to avoid at the age of seventeen and now that he was twenty-two, it was still difficult.

Sharon was sitting on the floor in the living room at the coffee table. On the edge of three of the sides were her stuffed animals, including Bubba. She was engaging in a pretend tea party with her toys. Sharon giggled, pouring some imaginary tea into their porcelain cups. Turning around to view of her father sitting in the kitchen, the little girl grabbed a tiny teacup from the table and ran to her father. Giving him the teacup, she wrapped her arm around her father's waist. Smiling, Paul pretended to drink the imaginary tea from the cup and gave his daughter an affectionate pat on the back. Leaning down, he gave her a kiss on the forehead.

There was the sound of a car pulling into the driveway, then the front door opening and closing.

"I have to get going," Paul said to his friend. "It's almost family time."

"Ok," Stephen replied, "Paul, if it means anything, I'd like to keep in touch. Sorry about the things I've said and done that made it so horrible that you couldn't talk to me back then. As I've said, a lot of the guys from the football, baseball, and basketball teams have been wanting to contact you. If there was anyone that was the heart and backbone of the teams, it was you. I can't speak for everyone, but I don't care if you're with Nell, I just want my buddy back."

"Sure, I'd like that too, pal," Paul said, his voice almost cracking; his eyes brimming with tears. "I'll give you a call back later." He hung up the phone.

Nell entered the kitchen. She appeared much more relaxed than he'd seen her in a while and even had more of a bounce to her steps. Nell's face was upturned, and her beautiful brown eyes sparkled, elating Paul's heart. She had that genuine smile that had been missing previously, bringing a smile to Paul's face.

Sharon rushed to her mother, wrapping her arms around her legs. Caressing the child's hair, Nell happily lifted Sharon up, resting the child on her hip.

"Hey, baby," Nell greeted Sharon, kissing her cheek. She approached Paul, giving him a deep kiss that sent heat radiating through his chest.

"Someone's in a good mood," Paul acknowledged. "What's the special occasion?"

"Well," Nell said, her voice bubbly, "The professor gave everyone the wrong test at first, but he, then, gave us the real test and I passed! In fact, all of us that had the tutoring with you passed! I aced it! Now I have a solid B in the class, thanks to you!"

"We should go out and celebrate," Paul said, his smile contagious. "I'm so happy for you! I knew you could do it! What do you feel like eating?"

"Honestly," Nell said, "After everything, a simple pizza at Camellia's Family Pizza would be so good right now!"

"So, cheese pizza," Paul snickered, giving her a thumbs up.

"Pizza," Sharon repeated, cheerfully.

Chapter 40

A week later, the phone began to ring. Paul shoved a few more bits of popcorn into his mouth, savoring its buttery taste. It was the evening, Sharon was put to bed, and Paul and Nell were watching a horror movie on the television set. Paul enjoyed watching those types of movies with Nell because her fears always made her a target of his late-night pranks. Nell was terrified of spiders, so when she least expected it, Paul would position his hands into a claw, slowly and lightly moving random fingertips somewhere along Nell's body. Nell fell for it every time, flinching her body closer to Paul's in surprise. Of course, it often resulted in Nell giving him an annoyed nudge or light smack on the arm.

Paul sauntered into the kitchen and pressed the phone against his ear.

"Hello?" Paul answered.

"Paul," the somewhat familiar voice said, "this is Mr. Jefferson, Nell's dad. Is Nell there?"

"*Mr.* Jefferson?" Paul exclaimed. "Yes, she is. I'll go and get her."

"Don't," Mr. Jefferson spoke. "Don't even bother. I only wanted to call and hear how she was doing."

"Wouldn't it be better if you talked to her yourself?" Paul asked.

"I don't need your smart-aleck response," Mr. Jefferson countered. "I only inquired about one thing that required a simple answer."

"Sorry, sir," Paul told him, "But all due respect, it would mean more to your daughter to hear directly from you."

"She wouldn't want to hear from me," Mr. Jefferson said. "Not after the way she left when she was staying here. My wife and other children are still upset as well."

There was a barely audible sound at the other end of the phone.

"All I ever wanted was for her to be successful," Mr. Jefferson continued. "My own parents struggled with the three children they had, which included me. We didn't have time to worry about school because we were busy trying to survive day to day. I've gone to bed hungry many a night, just so my younger brothers could eat. I promised myself that should I have my own children, they would never know what it was like to miss a meal or have opportunities taken away from them that could have made their lives easier. Can you imagine how it was for me to find out that my oldest didn't listen or learn anything from those experiences, after everything my wife and I've done to push her to get that high school diploma?"

"I can only imagine," Paul said. "By now, everyone's had more time to think about what occurred and it seems that you both want a peaceful resolve. Mr. Jefferson, my offer still stands for you to join us in our home at any time to drop by."

There was a long period of silence.

"Sir," Paul said, "this is a suggestion. If a phone call or visit won't work at this time, maybe a letter would be a better option. It's a start and can give you time to gather your thoughts."

"You think she would write back?"

"Maybe, but would you write back, if she did?"

"I would."

"Like I said, it's a start," Paul said. "Also, Mr. Jefferson, thanks…"

"For what?"

"Caring for Nell as much as you do and giving me a chance to talk to you. I hope that we can continue to talk more."

Chapter 41

"A bigger town would be more sustainable," Simon informed Paul, placing the documents neatly into his briefcase.

"I can't think of a town more deserving," Paul responded. "Sure, it's not perfect, but in time, I'm sure that the new store will help bring people closer together. After all, that's what my parents did at one point, only this time, it will be more inclusive."

After leaving his uncle's mansion, Paul parked his car to the nearest phone booth in town. He was still in the early stages of his plans that would take years, but he figured, it would be best to plan ahead. Even if things didn't work out, he already had his alternatives in mind.

Pressing his ear against the phone, he pushed the coins into the slot. He tilted his head back as he waited for the operator to connect him to the family that his own had sinned against years ago.

"Hello?" a woman's voice answered.

"Is Mrs. Reynolds in?" Paul asked.

"Unfortunately, no," the woman stated. "My mother passed away almost four years ago. I'm Shelly Reynolds by the way. May I ask who you are and why you are calling?"

"Don't hang up, but my name is Paul Boudreaux," Paul said. "I'm sorry for everything my family has done to yours. I was only a high school student back then and had nothing to do with what happened to your father or his store, honest!"

"Yeah," Shelly said, resentment in her tone. "Well, what is it that you want, Paul?"

"To apologize for their actions," Paul said. "I want to make amends, if I can."

"I wish that were possible," Shelly told him. "But you can't bring my parents back. My mother was never the same after my father's death. She died of a broken heart, you know. Sometimes, I wish I could do the same, but I have a young son that needs me. We're in the process of moving in with relatives until I can find work to get a fresh start somewhere else. I was supposed to become a manager for my father's store, but that never happened."

"Shelly, I still have a few more years until I finish business school in Alabama," Paul said. "I have plans to open a new family store in Magnolia, Louisiana. It's still in the planning stages, but if you want, I would like for you to be part of it, to make it into the store that both our parents wanted for our community: a place for everyone. I will reopen Sal's later, but for now, I want to focus on the newer store. It already has its own financial backing; it just needs the right people behind it. Would you like to join me and be open to a management position once the store opens? Furthermore, I'd like to hire you as a member of my planning team which will include a very substantial salary."

"How do you know if I would be any good for your store?"

"Because your family has values and were willing to go up against people like my grandfather."

"That would be a huge risk that I am not sure I am willing to take, but you seem to be sincere and apologetic. If Magnolia is more open to people like us, I'll be more than willing to work with you."

"Thank you," Paul said.

They exchanged numbers, conversing a little bit for what was to come later. After the phone call, Paul was not finished. He asked for the operator to connect him to a flower shop in Magnolia, Louisiana, to send pink lilies to the woman who had helped him and his wife as teens. The pink lilies were to be delivered weekly, for the remainder of her life, with a note that read:

With love, sending you some sugar

If lilies weren't available, Paul left instructions to give her the most beautiful flowers in the shop, regardless of the costs, funded by him.

When his calls had ended, Paul drove home, happy to see Nell and Sharon. He lifted Sharon from the ground, giving her a kiss on the cheek. Giggling, the little girl tilted her head back, puckering her lips, and giving him a kiss on the cheek.

"I love you," Sharon said, her voice loud.

"I love you too," Paul said giving her a tight squeeze. He turned to Nell, who was smiling. He wrapped his free arm around her. "Aaaaannnddd, I love you too, babe!" He chuckled giving her a smooch on the lips.

"I love you too, Paul," Nell said happily, returning the kiss.

About The Author

Regina N. Smith is an African American writer born and raised in Louisiana. She is the wife of a Vietnam veteran and comes from a family of educators and veterans. She writes books on bullying, interracial relationships, racial discrimination, child abuse, etc. In her spare time, Regina enjoys writing, genealogy, traveling, and returning lost and found objects to families.